The Boss Boycott
Maggie Linn Sharpe

Paperback Edition ISBN-13: 979-8-9923370-3-7

eBook Edition ISBN-13: 979-8-9923370-4-4

Cover design by Maggie Linn Sharpe.

Edited by: Lily Luchesi, Partners In Crime Book Services

Also by Maggie

The Songbird Cafe Series

To anyone thinking about changing course.

Your dreams and goals are allowed to change. You haven't failed. Following your heart means you've succeeded.

I HOPE YOU DON'T MIND ME SAYING

I THINK YOU'RE SO LOVELY

I HOPE YOU DON'T MIND ME STAYING

CAUSE I MIGHT NEVER LEAVE

WE COULD REWIND TO NOTHING

AND START AT THE BEGINNING

DON'T FORGET TO BREATHE

Saving Jane

Contents

Chapter One

Annie

I WAKE UP TO the sound of voices, disoriented and covered in a light sheen of sweat. Even when I'm wearing only a lightweight, baggy t-shirt, my childhood bedroom gets too warm at night for comfort during the hot months. It's late May now, so it's only going to get worse as the Ohio summer gets underway. Maybe I'll invest in a window air conditioner if I stay longer than a couple of weeks.

Mom swears she won't need my help longer than that, but I'm not so sure. A knee replacement is no joke, and she's struggling now that she's back home. Between the actual pain she's in and the side effects of the pain meds she's on, she's been out of it. I don't plan to head back to Chicago until I'm sure she's good on her own.

A pang of guilt hits me, just like it always does when I picture Mom sitting alone in this empty house, with no family here in Fort Starling to help her. Sure, she's got an excellent set of friends and coworkers at her law firm, but I'm the only blood relative she has left. There was no question that I'd come home to help her while she's recovering.

When I got the call that Mom would need surgery right away, I immediately started rearranging my schedule so I could come home to help her with the recovery. After taking a nasty fall at her dance exercise class that violently wrenched her knee, her doctor moved up the knee replacement she had planned for next year. Her friends took turns staying with her at the hospital until I could get there. They've been incredibly helpful, bringing us food, keeping her company, and helping with the house and yardwork.

Other than her awesome friends, my mom and I only have each other since my dad walked out on us when I was seven. We never heard from him again, and I've never bothered to look for him. Her parents died before I was born, and she was an only child, so it's been the two of us against the world. So, when I got the call, I loaded up my mermaid blue-green Honda Fit as soon as I could and hit the road back home to Fort Starling.

Right now, she needs help with just about everything. She can use a walker to get to the bathroom, but she needs help navigating the doors and maneuvering herself once she's there. When she's able to shower in a few days, that will be a whole new adventure.

Luckily, her bedroom is on the first floor of the small house where she has lived all my life. I cringe at the thought of getting her up the stairs in her current state. Her home office is upstairs, across the hall from my room, but she can set up shop at the dining room table when she goes back to work until she gets more comfortable with the stairs.

I sit up and check the time on my phone. It's only nine in the morning, so why is Mom's TV so loud? I drag myself out of bed and head down to check on her. I don't bother changing out of my ratty Ohio State tee before groggily stomping my way down the stairs.

Once I make sure she's good, refresh her ice packs, maybe get her some food if she's up to eating, I'll collapse back into bed for a couple more hours. I worked late last night catching up on the work that has piled up while I'm home. During the six-hour drive home yesterday, almost fifty emails arrived in my inbox, all of them needing my attention.

I'm technically using vacation time, but since the financial planning and investment firm I work for is one of the most high-profile firms in Chicago, there's no such thing as time off, regardless of what our HR policies say. Our clients are high maintenance and need massive amounts of hand-holding, making it nearly impossible to be truly out of office.

Of course, I also had to fight with Kevin, my jackass of a supervisor, just to take these couple of weeks to help my mom. He couldn't seem to get it through his head that my mom having emergency surgery was something I needed to come home for. He offered to reassign my clients while I was gone, but he's already started taking clients away from me. I didn't want to give him any room to take more.

Part of that is him doing his best to make things hard for me, as usual. We have a bit of... unfortunate history that has made working for him increasingly more difficult. I'm pretty sure he's trying to see how far he can push me before I break and quit. Not happening, asshole. I'm not giving up my entire career to get away from him.

I stumble tiredly into Mom's bedroom, where the voices seem to have quieted down. Her blackout curtains are drawn against the morning light, but the bedside lamp is on, as is the light in her en suite bathroom. I glance at her decorative fireplace, which holds her TV, and see that it's shut off.

Huh. I could have sworn I heard a man's voice.

I glance over to where she's reclining in bed; her face a mask of pain. She's got her knee propped up on a special pillow that looks like a giant wedge. Her blankets are all thrown off to the side. Surprisingly enough, she looks like she's changed her clothes, or at least her top. She squints at me and takes one glance at my bare legs before her eyes widen in shock.

"Annie Louise Martin, where are your pants? Or your bra? We have company!" she hisses through clenched teeth. I'm about to ask what the hell she's talking about when I hear a deep, familiar chuckle from the hallway behind me.

Fuck. I haven't seen my mortal enemy in a few years, but I'd recognize his snide voice anywhere.

"Oh, don't worry, Ms. Martin, it's nothing I haven't seen before. Right, Annie?"

I clench my eyes shut and ball my hands into fists for a second before turning to see Eric Reynolds staring down at me with a cocky smirk on his handsome face, a fresh icepack in his hands. He crosses to my mom and helps her place the icepack across her knee before turning back to look at me. His eyes connect with mine, and my stomach flips, like it always has. He's barely changed in the twelve years since we were college freshmen which is completely unfair. Why couldn't he have a beer belly and a receding hairline?

He styles his dark blonde hair to be slightly messy on top with the sides clipped short, and his eyes remain the same piercing blue I remember from college. His only sign of aging is a few small lines framing his eyes that only make him seem distinguished, the prick. He has a light shadow of stubble on his face, as if he shaved yesterday but skipped it this morning, making his strong jaw even more pronounced.

He's bigger than I remember. He was always tall, but his lanky body has filled out with muscle that was definitely not there when he was eighteen. We both stand still, staring at each other for a long moment, the atmosphere thickening between us like it always does.

"Excuse me?" my mother exclaims, snapping me out of my perusal of grown-up Eric.

"Eric's being an ass, as usual," I explain. "You remember my boyfriend Scott from freshman year?"

I can see from the look on her face that she doesn't. Honestly, I barely remember Scott, despite our months-long relationship. If it weren't for my unending war with his hot but dickish roommate, I might have forgotten him altogether.

"Uh, vaguely," she finally answers.

"Scott was my roommate freshman year, and Annie here was practically the unofficial extra roommate I never asked for. She was in our room all the time, eating our food, making a mess, and running around without enough clothing," Eric interjects.

"I did not!" I seethe. "You're just making shit up now!"

He's not making shit up. I did everything he said and more. I lived for pissing him off every chance I got freshman year. In fact, I dated Scott for longer than I intended, so I'd still have the chance to get under Eric's skin. I was a lot more interested in being a thorn in Eric's side than I was in breaking things off with Scott the douchebag. It's probably something I should discuss with a therapist at some point.

"Oh, bullshit, sweetheart," he says with an eye roll, knowing the fake endearment will set me off, just like it did in college.

I should probably examine the fact that my reaction to him should be more mature at thirty than it was at eighteen, but I'm too busy being filled with white-hot rage. Clearly, he hasn't matured any more than I have, either, since he's trying to bait me.

"I am not your sweetheart," I snap back. He's always called me that, usually just to get a rise out of me.

"You can rewrite history all you want. You and I both know you spent all your time in our room, soaking up the scraps of attention Scott was willing to give you," he snaps, crossing his arms.

"What the fuck are you even doing here?" I practically yell. He still has a way of getting directly under my skin. I've had enough of his smug, handsome face and his asshole attitude, made even more humiliating by the fact I'm not wearing pants or a bra. I don't like him having the upper hand like this. Between the shock of his appearance in my house and my lack of clothing, I am feeling way too vulnerable to keep this fight going.

"Annie!" my mom scolds. "Dr. Reynolds is my physical therapist. He owns the practice and was here getting me set up for the first couple of weeks of at-home care."

"It would have been nice if you told me you had PT coming this morning," I say through clenched teeth. "If I knew someone would be here, I would have gotten dressed before coming down."

"I thought I mentioned it," Mom mumbles tiredly and I cross my arms to cover my visibly hard nipples which only makes my shirt ride up higher on my thighs.

Eric smirks and gives me a slow, up-and-down perusal that I can feel in the pit of my stomach. He lingers on my bare legs before finishing his appraisal. The atmosphere between us thickens even more, making it hard to catch my breath. It's hard to tell whether I'd like to kill him or drag him to a room my mother is not in and beg him to fuck me senseless.

That's always been my dilemma with Eric. The tension between us is insane, but the hatred has always been a little bit stronger. Strong enough to keep me from throwing myself at him. I shake my head to remove that disturbing line of thought, and his mouth turns up into a wolfish grin, as if he could read my mind.

"Not a big deal." Eric shrugs, like he wasn't just checking me out a moment before. "Like I said, it's nothing I haven't seen before. Besides, that was over a decade ago, and it looks like time hasn't been kind to all of us, huh?"

I gasp loudly and ball my hands into fists, fighting the urge to throat-punch him. My vision goes red; I can't be in this room with him anymore. I give him one last scathing glance, turn on my heel, and march out of the room. What an ass, but I guess I shouldn't be surprised. From the moment he found me in his room after I started dating Scott, he's been a total dick to me.

We end up fighting any time we're in the same room. Every couple of years, we run into each other at some party or other. One of my best friends, Jessie, is married to his friend Dan, so we end up invited to some of the same things. I do my best to avoid him, but we inevitably break down into snide comments and insults once we've each had a few drinks.

Seeing him here may have been a surprise, but us falling into our old habits of hostility and cheap insults is par for the course. I'm embarrassed that my mom witnessed it all. I know I'll be getting an earful about it later on today, but for now, I've had enough.

I stomp my way up to my room and slam the door for good measure before flopping back onto the bed, closing my eyes. I am not running on enough sleep to be dealing with assholes like Eric Reynolds. I need to go back to sleep and forget about this waking nightmare. But when I finally drift off, it's with the image of Eric's striking blue eyes lingering in my mind.

My ringing phone wakes me. Who the hell is calling me? Don't they know texting is the only appropriate form of contact? I find my phone to see Jessie's name flashing on the screen. She's one of the select few people I will answer a phone call for, plus we usually schedule regular FaceTimes, so an unannounced call means trouble.

"Hey, babes. What's up?" My voice is scratchy with sleep. I clear my throat and sit up in bed.

"Ugh, Leena is falling apart. I think it's gonna take both of us to turn this one around. I'm heading over to the Songbird here in a little while to do damage control. Can I call you on speaker when I get there?"

"I'll do you one better. I'm in town, and I can meet you over there." I smile into the phone at her silence. There are not a ton of ways to shut Jessie up, but that seems to have worked.

"Bitch. Why did you not tell anyone?" she screeches into the phone.

Matching her joking endearment with my own, I reply, "Skank. I'm here taking care of my mom. She had emergency knee surgery, and it's been a rough couple of days."

Jessie sighs noisily into the phone, aggravated by the surprise and my insistence on handling everything myself. It's a regular debate for us, especially since she and Leena are both back in Fort Starling permanently.

"We could have helped out if we knew. You've got to tell us these things, A."

"It's fine! I've got it handled," I mumble into the phone. Asking for help has never been my forte.

"Well. Okay. I'm still pissed you didn't tell us... but I'm also thrilled you're here to help with the Leena situation."

Leena is the third member of our trio. After discovering our mutual love of reading and musical theatre, one day in the middle school library, we've been inseparable ever since. We even all went to college together before going our separate ways. We knew college could be one of the last chances we would have to all be together before life took over.

I stayed in Columbus for a few years before I moved to Chicago to chase a bigger finance scene than Ohio offered. I landed an entry-level finance job and have worked my way up to my current spot. Work-life balance was supposed to be a little easier to find once I got this last promotion, but the workload only increased. Over here, living the dream, working seventy-hour weeks and eating takeout in my apartment alone most nights.

Jessie met her husband Dan in our freshman year of college when he was a senior, and they've been together ever since. He's the catcher for the local professional baseball team, the Fort Starling Flash. When he was first drafted, they dated long distance so she could finish school, and got married right after we graduated. They moved around a bunch when Dan was traded a few times before coming back to Fort Starling, where they've been for the last few years.

Leena's had a rough go of it since college. Right after school, she moved to Columbus for a while. She was engaged to an asshole for a bit and we thought for sure she'd marry the guy but that was before moving home to take care of her Gram, who raised her. After Gram passed away a couple of years ago, Leena dumped the jackass and opened the Songbird Cafe and Bar. It's a coffee shop in the morning and a bar at night that hosts infamous open mic nights twice a week.

Getting out of bed, I get dressed while Jessie updates me on Leena and Bailey, the Flash pitcher Jessie set Leena up with a few months back. It sounds like shit hit the fan yesterday between them, but I think it's fixable based on everything Leena's told me over FaceTime.

"Jess, I'm leaving now. I'll meet you at the bar."

"Thanks, babes! But also, we're not done talking about your inability to ask for help when you need it."

I roll my eyes. That's what she thinks. I'm done talking about it. I rush Jessie off the phone and let my mom know I'm heading out. Fixing other people's problems is far preferable to paying any attention to my own. Time to go take care of my best friend.

IT'S BEEN A LOVELY couple of weeks home, but with my mom mostly back on her feet and Leena all squared away (that's a whole other story for another time), it's time for me to head back to Chicago. I'm grudgingly packing up my suitcase so that I can get an early start in the morning.

When I first moved away, it was always bittersweet to head back to Chicago after a visit at home. I miss my mom and my friends, but I loved the hustle and challenge of the city. Now returning feels a lot more bitter than sweet, but I'm not sure what I could even do about it. I push the thought aside as I hear Mom clomping her way up the stairs with her cane.

"You good?" I call, making sure she doesn't need help.

"I'm good. Gotta practice getting up these stairs. I'm gonna hate working at that fucking table."

I huff out a laugh as she enters my room. She hobbles her way over to my bed and sinks down, getting the weight off of her knee.

"How are you feeling? Doing okay without the heavy drugs?"

"Yeah, I only need them at night now. I gotta wean off of them so I can work next week. My case load is pretty light right now, but one of my clients' hearings is coming up next month, so I need to get going on the prep work."

I nod. I'm glad she's getting back to her normal self, but I'll admit it was nice to be needed for these couple of weeks. No one in Chicago needs me.

"Annie Lou, what's up? You seem... I don't know... sad somehow? Aren't you looking forward to heading back?" She's always refused to refer to Chicago as "home," and even though I've lived there for over five years, I don't either. Fort Starling is home.

"I guess I enjoyed being home. Things are... not the best at work, and since all I do is work..." I trail off, not wanting to admit how much I hate my job these days.

Mom nods. "You can always move home, you know that, right? You always have a place here. We'd all be happy to have you."

"I know. I'm not ready to give up yet. I'll let you know if I get to that point, though."

"Good. I love you, Annie Lou," she says as she limps over to wrap me in a big hug. She always manages to make me feel protected like a little kid, despite the fact that I've stood several inches taller than her five-foot-two stature since I was in the sixth grade.

"Love you too, Mama," I murmur into her hair. She hobbles herself back down the stairs to go to bed, and I replay our conversation.

Could I move home? What would I do here? Why does it feel like I'd be giving up, failing if I came crawling home? Why do I kind of want to do it, anyway?

I can't. At least not yet. I'm not ready to give up on the career that I've been building for years just because I was dumb enough to sleep with the boss.

But, man, will I miss being home.

Chapter Two

Eric

Apparently, this is the week for frustrating interactions. First, I ran into Annie Fucking Martin yesterday. I didn't think anything of it when I read the last name on Sherrie Martin's intake paperwork. It's a pretty common last name, and while Fort Starling isn't a huge city, it's not a small town either.

It was a shock seeing her, especially seeing so much of her, that I almost lost track of finishing my patient's appointment. Annie's always had a distracting and frustrating presence. From the moment we met freshman year, she was a constant mix of enticing and infuriating.

Now, my bio dad's name flashes across my phone screen right as I pull into the lot for my office. I do not have the energy to deal with him first thing in the morning, but I pull my hand through my hair, gripping the strands and tugging at them before I hit answer. He'll keep calling if I don't.

"Hi, Steve. What's up?" I say shortly into the phone. If he's calling me, he wants something, so it's better to get down to it.

"Hey there, Eric. How's it going, man?"

"I'm fine. How are you?" I've learned to keep it short and sweet since he's probably not actually listening to my answer. I'm not one of his clients who can make him money.

"Oh, I can't complain. Hey, I was wondering. Now that you're a PT for the Flash, are you able to get season tickets? Maybe some comped games? I've got some clients that are big Flash fans."

There it is. It's always something with him.

"Uh, I'm not sure. I can look into it. It's just part-time working with a few of the guys, so I don't know."

"I'm sure they can spare you some tickets for keeping their guys in playing shape. You let me know what you hear, alright?"

"Yeah, will do." My jaw is clenched tight, like it always is while talking to Steve.

"Okay, I'll talk to you soon, kiddo!"

And just like that, he's gone, off to the next person who can give him something. In hindsight, it makes total sense why my moms weren't interested in him being an actual parent when they used his sperm for me and my sister.

At eighteen, though, I insisted I wanted to get to know him. My moms supported me, and let's just say it did not go well. I expected a dad like all my friends had but got an uninterested and self-absorbed man-child instead.

My older sister, Jenna, was the smart one and decided she wasn't interested in getting to know him. She's happy to think of him as her sperm donor and nothing more. They've met a few times, but I don't think she talks to him outside of the occasional family gathering he comes to.

It's taken years and a lot of therapy for me to be in an okay place when it comes to my relationship with Steve. Now, I don't expect much, knowing he won't give much. He's not really my dad, just a guy who supplied half of my DNA. Affirmations I have to repeat to myself whenever I get the stab of disappointment that comes from interacting with him.

I yank my hands through my hair again, trying to make the strands look more orderly and less like I've been electrocuted. Pushing both Steve and Annie out of my mind, I head into my office to start my day. I have to start figuring out what's going on with the practice bookkeeping today, and I'll need a clear mind to deal with numbers.

"WHAT THE FUCK IS wrong with this?" I say out loud to my empty office for what has to be the hundredth time in the last couple of weeks since I started digging into the practice's bookkeeping. My week of frustration that started with Annie's appearance is shaping up to be a month of frustration if the accounting software has anything to say in the matter.

My office manager of five years retired last month, and the more I dig into the books, the more I realize that I should have been paying closer attention all along. Nothing makes sense. Some clients haven't been billed, some were billed too much, and some records are completely missing. The tax paperwork is a total mess.

I'm not sure how the reports Vicki used to print out for me even existed with the mess I'm finding in the accounting software. She had to have found the information somewhere. Or, the more likely explanation, she was making it up. I have no idea, and the impending sense of dread is starting to settle in my stomach like a pile of rocks.

I rub at my eyes to keep the numbers from blurring together. I'm gonna need to hire a new office manager who has some bookkeeping experience as soon as possible. A knock at the open office door signals my Physical Therapist Assistant, Tasha, popping her blonde head in.

"Hey Eric, Sherrie Martin is here, and I know you wanted to check in on her progress today."

"Thanks, Tash, I'll be right there."

"Okie dokie!" she singsongs as she heads back out to the floor. Tasha is a perpetual ball of sunshine and a great PTA. She interned here with me while she was in school, and I offered her a full-time job as soon as she was ready. She's kept this place running while I muddle through the business side of things, even though I'd rather be out on the floor with her, working with patients. I don't think I realized how much admin work I'd need to do when I opened my own practice.

I let out a deep breath before heading out to the floor to check on Annie's mom. I can't help but think about that day at Sherrie's house and my latest run-in with Annie. It was a pretty standard interaction for us, full of rude comments and insults. But this time it was embarrassing to have it happen in front of my patient, who also happens to be Annie's mother. I can't imagine she loved the way I spoke to her daughter. I'm not particularly proud of myself.

I meet all kinds of people in my line of work, but no one in my thirty years has ever gotten under my skin like Annie Martin. The first time we met, I thought I had found my dream girl, but it turns out she was more like my nightmare. In college, we fought constantly, always doing our level best to piss off the other. After a while, it became like a game to find out how much I could push her.

In twelve years, not much has changed, it seems. I still got that same rush of adrenaline from fighting with her. If I'm being honest, that adrenaline is always paired with a decent dose of lust, and I had to drop my messenger bag over the front of my body to hide the evidence from Annie and her mom.

It doesn't help that Annie's only gotten hotter with age. My comment about her not aging well was a straight-up lie. She was pretty at eighteen, but now she's drop-dead gorgeous. With her long toned legs on display and her perky tits showing through her t-shirt I couldn't help but rake my eyes over her body. Even with her light brown hair piled into a messy bun and not a stitch of make-up, she's the most beautiful girl I've ever seen. I got a whiff of her familiar orange blossom and cinnamon scent as she stormed out that took me right back to college.

And just like back in college, once she left the room, I was hit with the familiar wave of regret and guilt. When we're in the heat of the fight, it's easy to say shitty things to her, but the aftermath never feels good. I clench my fists as I walk out of the back office, still pissed at myself for the things I said a couple of weeks ago.

Was it necessary for me to do this same juvenile shit? We aren't in college anymore and she's not blowing me off for my douchebag roommate. There is no excuse for being such a jackass, no matter how tempting it is to piss her off. Or how stunning she is to watch when I succeed.

I shake off thoughts of Annie as I hit the floor to check in with Tasha and Sherrie. Sherrie is doing her reps of one of the mobility stretches we do for knee replacements as Tasha watches and keeps count. Sherrie looks so much like an older version of Annie that it steals my breath for a moment as I approach.

"Hey Sherrie, how ya feeling?"

"Doing alright. Glad to be done with the walker and down to just a cane."

I grab the iPad from Tasha to check over Sherrie's most recent measurements. "Everything seems good here. We're on track for you to have another week here in the office, then you'll be all set."

"I'm ready. Now that I won't have Annie around doing everything for me at home, I'll be getting up and around more and more."

"Oh. Annie's heading back to Chicago?" I ask, pretending to be casual about it. Somehow, I'm both relieved and disappointed I won't be running into her again.

"She left this morning. She's probably about an hour from the city at this point," she replies with a frown and a glance at her watch.

"You okay?"

"Oh, yeah." She waves her hand at me and smiles with a rueful expression on her face. "I miss her when she's gone. I'd love for her to move home, but... Anyway, I'm sure you're just fine with her living far away, hmm?"

My face flushes with shame as Sherrie raises her eyebrows. I study the ground and shift from foot to foot. When I look up, I find her watching me. Her eyes twinkle with amusement, enjoying my obvious distress. Tasha's gaze bounces back and forth between me and Sherrie, curiosity shining on her young face.

"Right, about that. Um... will you tell Annie... uh, just tell her I'm sorry for what I said?" I murmur. I rake my hands through my hair, embarrassed.

Sherrie studies me for a long moment with a calculating look on her face. She's clearly still trying to figure out what kind of history I have with her daughter. I wonder what Annie told her. I swallow hard and clench my jaw as she stares me down.

"Wouldn't you like to tell her that yourself? I can give you her number," she offers.

I shake my head quickly. "No, it's probably best if you pass along the message. We're likely to fight some more." Plus, the idea of being able to contact Annie feels too tempting for some reason, but I'm not about to tell Sherrie that. "She'd probably block my number instantly."

"Mmhmm," she replies, still staring me down. Sherrie Martin must be an amazing attorney because she's intimidating as hell. I can understand where Annie gets her fiery energy. Finally, she nods as if she's decided, "Alright, Eric. I'll pass the message along."

"Thanks. Have a good one," I say and get the fuck out of there, and go back to staring at my accounts and spreadsheets without a clue how to fix them.

As I drive home later that night, I'm still thinking about Sherrie and kicking myself for being such a dick to Annie. I spent so much of freshman year both pissed at her and pining for her. Now, here I had yet another chance to give her a new impression of me, and I stuck with the same old one. I blew it with her. Again.

Parked in my driveway, I lean my head back against the seat and close my eyes, taking a moment to picture Annie as she looked that morning. I resolve right then and there. If I get another chance, I'm not going to mess it up.

Tenth time's the charm, right?

Chapter Three

Annie

Seven Months Later

"I DON'T UNDERSTAND THE problem, Kevin," I practically growl into my steering wheel as I'm driving across the Ohio border. The snow is picking up speed, and I have to turn up my windshield wipers to keep up. The stormy gray sky perfectly matches my mood while talking to Kevin through my car speakers.

"I cleared this time off with HR weeks ago. You know my mom's having her second knee replacement surgery next week. I'll be available for any client questions over Christmas and back after New Year's. What's the issue?"

Rage starts to bubble under my skin, and I take a deep breath to calm down. He's trying to piss me off, to get me to make a mistake. My temper has already gotten me into way too much trouble with this asshole and I can't afford more.

"The issue is that your performance has been slipping for months now." Kevin's arrogant voice intones. "Your billables have dropped consistently month by month."

"That's because you keep taking my clients and giving them to Serena," I say with clenched teeth. It's hard to keep my billables up when he's undermining me at every turn and giving my clients to his girlfriend.

"Don't be mad that Serena's a better closer," he taunts.

Serena's a better something, alright. She's better at pretending that Kevin's decent in bed. She's better at stroking his ego and playing the perfect little work wife. She's the embodiment of mean girl energy, and we never got along. Even before all of the Kevin-induced drama. Now, Kevin's been steadily off-loading my clients to her slowly as punishment for losing my damn temper with him in the office.

I'm not proud of the way I reacted. I could have been a cool professional and let his dismissal roll off my back, but I've never been great at handling rejection well. Something about it sends me into a total tailspin, and I see red. Blame it on the daddy issues I have yet to work through.

So, instead, I lost my damn temper and called him out in the middle of our office. I admitted to faking any orgasms he thought he provided. I did it loudly, in front of other co-workers. Is it any wonder he's trying to push me out of the firm now?

"So, what are you suggesting?" I ask in a clipped tone.

"Well, I talked to the managing partner, and she agrees we should go ahead and reassign your current clients while you're on leave."

Fuck. I shouldn't be surprised. This shouldn't sting as much as it does. *Don't cry until you're off the call.*

"So, you want to reassign my clients for the three weeks that I'll be gone? That seems like a lot of work just to reassign them back." I hold my breath, waiting for him to drop the hammer that I know is coming next.

"Well, Catherine thought it would be best if you took a longer leave. She thinks three months would be better." I can practically hear the giddiness in his tone. He's been working toward this moment for the past year, since I told him I wouldn't have had to fake orgasms if he wasn't boring in bed.

"So, you and your mom are just deciding that I'm taking a three-month leave?" I can't resist referring to Catherine, our firm's managing partner, as his mom instead of her name. I know it makes him crazy.

"The *managing partner* thinks it would be good for you to take some time to regroup and decide if your heart's really in this business." Kevin sneers back at me. I definitely struck a nerve.

"Let me guess. You don't have actual cause to fire me, so you're giving me this bullshit about taking time and when that time is done, there won't be any clients for me to take over." I'm losing my tenuous grip on my temper quickly now. This call needs to end before I straight-up quit, or start calling him names, or comment on his average sized dick and his inability to use it well. "I'm assuming this is a paid leave?"

"Your base salary, yes, but you won't qualify for commissions since you won't have any clients on your caseload," Kevin clips back. I'm sure he's about to do cartwheels across his office.

"Fine. I'll see you in three months." I just barely manage to hang up the phone before I burst into tears, the frustration and anger pouring out. Three months' salary is better than nothing to figure out where I go from here. It'll at least pay for my Chicago apartment while I decide if I still want to live there.

I crank the Taylor Swift playlist I have going and focus on driving. I take a deep breath and wipe the tears from my eyes as I speed down the highway through the falling snow towards home. Looks like I'm about to have an extended stay in Fort Starling.

INSTEAD OF GOING STRAIGHT to my mom's house, I decide to stop by the Songbird Cafe and Bar to see if Leena is working. It occurs to me as I'm parking that she might not be. Now that she's moved in with her hunky baseball player boyfriend, she doesn't spend as much time at the Songbird.

I open the door and take a look around at the bar that I've come to love in the couple of years since Leena opened it. The Songbird Cafe and Bar is a large, open rectangular room with a bar running along the right side of the room, with open back barstools along the front.

Seating is a mix of cozy chairs and couches, with high-top tables scattered throughout the room. They have a few racks of donated new and used books that operate like a Little Free Library along the left side of the room. I love to visit, find a new book to read, and a comfy chair to relax in when I'm home visiting.

Towards the back of the bar, there's a barista station that handles all the morning cafe drinks with a pastry case that still has a few treats from local bakeries, despite being late in the afternoon. A mirrored wall displays an assortment of liquor and mixers for the evening crowd. The stage, complete with microphone, electric keyboard, and speaker system, sits in the left corner for open mic nights. It looks like Leena's been setting up for one tonight.

It's only four in the afternoon, so there aren't many people here. They do most of their business in the early morning for the coffee crowd and in the late evening for the alcohol drinkers. I stroll in and take a seat on a barstool. I hear someone moving things around in the back kitchen area.

"I'll be out in just a sec," Leena's voice calls.

"Take your time, babes!" I yell back. There's a beat of silence before she screams and launches herself through the doorway.

"Annie! What are you doing here?" she screeches. "Why do you never tell me when you're gonna be home?"

"Because I love the reaction I get when I surprise you, silly!"

She folds me into a hug and I sink into her, letting some of the tension from my fucked up professional life seep away. God, it's good to be home.

"What the hell are you doing home, Annie Lou? Oh my god, are you here for the holidays?" Leena asks using my childhood nickname, as she still has me locked in her hug.

The girls only bust out that nickname when they're being sentimental, which makes sense. I haven't seen Leena in person since I was here seven months ago, and I rarely get to come home for the holidays with my demanding job. We talk a ton on FaceTime and we text updates, but to actually be together is amazing.

"My mom's having her second knee replacement next week, so I took time off to come help."

"She's doing it right before Christmas?"

"She wanted to get it in before her deductible resets at the end of the year. With the other knee in May, this one's practically free. Plus, she says she has more downtime at work this time of year, so it makes more sense to use it for recovery if she isn't going to be working anyway." I shrug and shoot Leena a grin. "Basically, she's a workaholic."

"Like mother, like daughter," Leena snarks at me with her eyebrows raised.

"Ouch. Rude. I mean, you're not wrong but... rude."

Leena laughs and hugs me again. "You can always call me if Sherrie needs help, but fuck, I'm glad you're here!" She beams at me. It's good to see her so happy.

There was a long time after her Gram died and her engagement to her asshole of an ex ended that we were all worried about Leena, so it's wonderful to see her thriving. "How long are you in town for? Please, tell me we can have some girls' nights while you're here?"

"Well... I'm actually here until sometime in March." I say with a grimace, recalling my conversation with Kevin. "You remember the asshole boss I told you about?"

"Yeah, wasn't he giving your clients to his office bimbo?" she asks, scowling. "The one that was such a bitch to you?"

"Yep. And now he's convinced the managing partner, aka his Mommy, to put me on a three-month leave while office Barbie takes over my entire caseload," I grumble.

Leena gasps, outraged on my behalf. "You've got to be fucking kidding me?" she huffs angrily. "What are you supposed to do without a job for three months?"

"Well, they'll still be paying me my base salary, so that will at least cover the rent and utilities on my apartment. I'll probably pick up some side accounting jobs while I'm here. Also, I was thinking... is anyone living in the apartment here?"

"Not at the moment. It's been empty since I moved in with Bailey."

"Once my mom is back on her feet in a couple of weeks, I was hoping maybe I could move in here? Mom's house is so small, and I'd rather have my own space to stew about my dumpster fire of a career," I admit.

"Of course! I'll get it all cleaned up and aired out for you. You can stay here as long as you need!" Leena wraps me in another warm hug. If my career had to go up in flames, I'm sure as shit glad I was already coming home when it happened.

"It's open mic tonight! You sticking around?" Leena asks hopefully. "Jessie and some guys from the team are planning on coming by, so it'll be a fun time. Maybe take your mind off everything?"

"You know, that sounds like a perfect plan. I'm gonna swing by and visit with Mom for a bit and unload my car. I'll get changed and head back over here around seven?"

"Sounds perfect!" Leena beams back at me.

It really does. A night of drinking and singing with my closest friends sounds like just what I need.

"MOM?" I CALL OUT as I enter the house through the side kitchen door that opens from our carport. At least I won't have to clear snow off my car while I'm living here. It'll be weird driving my own car everywhere instead of taking a train.

"Annie?" I hear her call back from upstairs. Her slow pace down the stairs reminds me why I came home in the first place. She'll feel so much better when that second knee isn't giving her so many problems. "Hey, baby girl! Are you just getting into town?"

She looks at the clock on the stove as she pulls me into a hug. All these hugs from my favorite people are really helping my outlook on life. I smile down at my petite mother and squeeze her back. While I got my toffee brown hair and brown eyes from my mom, and we have very similar features, I inherited some height from my sperm donor of a dad.

"Nah, I stopped by the Songbird to see Leena for a bit before I came here," I explain. She nods and takes a seat at the small kitchen table.

"How's Leena doing?"

"She's great! The bar's doing well, and she's living with her super-star pitcher boyfriend. She seems really happy!" I say with a big smile.

"That's so good to hear. I know she had a rough patch there for a while after Lizzie passed," she says with a sad smile. My mom always loved Leena's Gram. We spent a lot of holidays with them since it was just the two of us and the two of them. Jessie would usually sneak away from whatever stuffy holiday parents her parents were throwing to join us. Losing Gram hit us all pretty hard, although not as hard as it hit Leena.

"So...Kevin finally pulled the trigger and sabotaged me." I drop the bomb nonchalantly, knowing my mom understands exactly how big of a deal the slow death of my career has been.

"Shit. What did that ass-weasel do?" she snaps.

I let out a deep sigh. "He convinced the partners to put me on a three-month leave and gave all the rest of my clients to Serena," I explain sadly. "I'm pretty sure they'll claim not to have clients for me, even if I decide to go back. Giving up and quitting feels like letting Kevin win, but I'm probably done there, so I'll be job hunting."

"Fucking hell," she swears with a scowl. I come by my potty mouth honestly. "So will you be job hunting in Chicago or..."

Mom has been wanting me to move home for years, so it's no surprise that she's hoping this will push me to stay. Honestly, at this point, it doesn't feel like Chicago has much left for me, but to move home also low-key feels like a failure.

"I don't know, Mom," I say tiredly. "This all went down today while I was driving, so I think I'm still processing it. For today, I'm going to put on a fun outfit and meet up with Leens and Jess at the Songbird for open mic night."

"Oh, that sounds fun! That's a perfect way to spend your first night home!" she says excitedly.

I don't mention my plan to move into the apartment over the bar yet. We'll save that discussion for another day. For now, it's time to put on some going-out clothes so that I can force myself into a better mood. I'm determined to have a good night and forget about my career issues for the night.

MY DRESS FITS ME like a glove. It's a fabulous deep blue color, and it's made of a slinky material that clings to every curve. The vee of the neckline dips low, making my smallish boobs look amazing. I curled my hair and gave myself a smoky eye to finish out the sexy-glam style I was going for. I already feel a little bit stronger.

"Whoa, baby!" Leena exclaims as I walk up to the bar. "Shit, A., you look hot!"

"Thanks, babes!" I smile back at her. "I figured getting all dolled up would help me get my mind off things."

"Well, damn, you really went for it." She pauses and looks deep in thought for a moment. "I'm trying to think of which single guys are coming with Bailey and Dan tonight. You're going to have to beat them off."

I smirk at her unintended innuendo and raise my eyebrows. Leena points at me.

"Hey! You know I didn't mean it like that!" she says with a laugh. "I'm not sure any of the guys coming tonight are your speed, anyway."

I shrug. I'm not particularly interested in hooking up with a baseball player. Jocks have never been my type. I'll take a brainy, bookish guy any day. At this point, I'm not interested in hooking up with anyone. I'm so tired of casual dating and one-night stands. It's part of why my brain so thoroughly latched on to the idea of Kevin, even if the reality wasn't quite what I was looking for.

Leena pours me a drink, and we sit chit-chatting about what songs we should sing during the open mic night. I'm not nearly the singer Leena is, and I can only play a few songs on the guitar, but I don't mind getting up to perform now and then. Growing up obsessed with musical theatre like we did, we got very used to singing whenever and wherever. All three of us were in the choir from middle school on.

Leena gasps as the door opens. She looks at me with wide eyes and cringes. Before I can turn to see who's walking into the bar, Leena grabs my arm, pulling my attention to her face.

"Fuck. I'm so sorry. I totally forgot that Bailey invited Eric," she murmurs. "Shit, shit, shit. I'm sorry, Annie. I know you hate each other."

"What are you talking about, Leens?" I ask, racking my brain for which Eric she's talking about, and then it hits me. There's only one Eric I know that Leena would apologize about. I freeze in my seat as a very tall person comes up beside me.

"Well, fancy seeing you here," Eric says in his taunting tone.

This is the absolute last thing I need tonight. I don't have the energy to fight with Eric after everything today. I summon the strength to glance up at him, and my heart flutters as I find him smiling down at me.

A real, friendly smile, like he's happy to see me, that sends waves of confusion through me. This man doesn't smile at me. He sneers.

What the fuck is happening?

Chapter Four

Eric

IT'S BEEN SIX OR seven months since I've seen Annie, and she looks even better than ever. She's surprised to see me, which tells me Leena didn't warn her I'd be here tonight. Lucky for me, Bailey told me earlier that Annie was in town and was going to be hanging with us at the Songbird, so I was able to mentally prepare.

Even with the forewarning, I'm not ready for how gorgeous she is. The slinky blue dress she's wearing looks incredible, and the dark makeup she has around her eyes makes the caramel color of her irises appear golden in the dim light of the bar. She has her light brown hair down around her shoulders in curls. She's a goddamn knock-out and, this time, I'm determined not to be a total dick to her.

"Well, fancy seeing you here," I say as I sidle up next to her at the bar. Her body stiffens, and she looks like she's preparing for a fight before she looks up at me. I give her my most genuine smile, and I can see her falter in her tracks. *Jesus*, I must really be an asshole if just a genuine smile is a foreign concept.

"Eric," she says in a clipped tone with a polite nod.

I expect her to follow up with something snarky, but it looks like she's attempting to be on her best behavior, too. We might actually get somewhere.

"You look nice tonight." I smile down at her again. I swear I said it genuinely, but her jaw clenches.

"Listen, man. I've had one of the shittiest days ever, so can we not do this tonight?" she snaps. "I don't have the energy to fight with you."

She looks so defeated, I feel a pang in my chest. I'm filled with the overwhelming desire to help her, fix whatever is making her act like someone killed her damn puppy. The urge to protect Annie is relatively new, but I don't hate it.

"Annie, I was being sincere," I say pleadingly. "You look beautiful. I wasn't trying to pick a fight. Is... there anything I can do to help?"

She freezes and stares me down for a long moment. Just when I think she might soften, she rolls her eyes and huffs out a sigh. Without another word, she hops down from her barstool and walks down to join the other ladies at the end of the bar.

Shit. How did this go wrong already? Getting on her good side is going to be harder than I thought. A beer thunks down on the bar in front of me, and I glance up to see Bailey giving me a sympathetic look. We've been good friends for a few years now, so he knows all about my history with Annie. I'm sure Leena has given him the inside scoop from Annie, whatever that might be.

"Saw all that, did you?" I ask grumpily. "I swear I was trying to be nice for once."

"I know." He nods. "I also know that she's had a terrible day and that she's not used to you being nice to her. Keep trying. She'll come around." He clinks his beer to mine and walks down to stand next to Leena. I watch as he leans in and kisses her behind the ear. She turns and gives him a beaming smile. Something rare for someone as snarky and deadpan as Leena.

A pang of... something...makes my heart clench in my chest. It's not exactly jealousy, but there's a sharp edge of longing to it. I'm happy for Bailey and Leena, glad that two people I admire so much have found each other. The older I get, the more I want something like that.

I was happy to mess around in my twenties. If I wanted a hookup, there were a handful of lovely ladies I could call. Now that I've crossed thirty, I'm not interested in the casual hookup life anymore. I want something more meaningful. Lasting. But so far, attempts at dating have been stale and boring. I haven't checked the apps for months, with everything I'm dealing with at the office. I let out a deep sigh as I take a long pull from my beer.

"Rough day?" I hear a deep voice say from the other side of me. I turn to find Fred Chambers sitting on the barstool next to me. He's a well known businessman and accountant in Fort Starling. When I was opening my practice, he helped me fill out the unending pile of paperwork that came with starting my own business.

Fred's in his mid-seventies and loves to come to Songbird's open mic nights to perform. He usually likes to choose off-the-wall song options that have made him a crowd favorite. Tonight, he's decked out in a red and green suit with bedazzling on the lapels. His white hair and the goatee that he's grown in recently give him the vibes of a modern, skinny Santa.

I bite the inside of my cheek to hide my smile as I offer my hand. "Mr. Chambers, how are you?"

"Oh, can't complain. The wife and I are in good health and both retired. All the kids and grandkids are doing well." He gives me a cheerful smile. He studies my face for a moment before adding, "I'm guessing from your weary sigh, things are less than fantastic with you?"

"I'm glad you're doing well. I'm... doing okay. Just feeling melancholy tonight." I shrug and gulp my beer. "I've actually been meaning to call you. We've made a bit of a mess of the books at the practice, and I could use some help."

"I can stop by sometime later this week to take a peek, but if it's gonna be a bit of a project, I'll have to give you some names of folks to call. Gail and I are taking off for a tour of Europe just after Christmas."

"That sounds like fun! I'd appreciate any guidance on what or who I need to fix the mess." I wince, thinking about the state of my business, which only gets more confusing the more I try to untangle things. "The office manager I hired a few years back swore she had bookkeeping experience and was sure what she was doing, and I'm ashamed to admit I didn't stay on top of it. Now things are completely wrecked and I can't figure it out."

"I'll come over Friday afternoon if that works for you. We'll get it figured out." He gives me another grandfatherly smile and a pat on my back. "Looks like I'm up."

He hops off his bar stool and makes his way up to the stage as Leena hops down. I missed whatever song she sang while I was chatting with Fred, but I'm sure it was a slow, sad one. She favors those even though she's in a good place with Bailey.

"Good evening, folks. Since we're deep into the holiday season now, I thought it only fitting to go with a Christmas classic." Fred grins into the microphone as the opening notes of Mariah Carey's "All I Want for Christmas Is You" play over the speakers. The crowd screams and whistles their approval along with a large dose of laughter.

Fred sings his heart out, but it's his dance moves that really make the performance. I'm guessing one of his granddaughters helped him choreograph the routine, complete with shoulder shimmies and hip shaking. The whole bar sings along with him, dancing in their seats. Leave it to Fred to bring the Christmas spirit to open mic night.

When he finishes, he takes an exaggerated bow. I've got to say, the old man rocked it, and the crowd seems to agree with me. There are smiles on almost every face in the room. Including a certain gorgeous brunette in a beautiful blue dress, sitting at the other end of the bar from me.

Feeling a little lighter knowing I've got help on the way for my practice, I make my way down the bar toward my friends, determined to try again to make a better impression on Annie. My luck holds out, and there's an open spot next to her at the bar. She rolls her eyes as I plop onto the barstool.

"Are you still here?"

"Just enjoying open mic night, sweetheart." I shoot her a smirk, and she stiffens at the casual endearment I've always used for her. I know it makes her crazy, and I can't resist.

"I'm *not* your sweetheart." She clips out her usual response. Her words are cold, but her eyes flash with heat. I suddenly realize I'm an idiot for trying to go straight from antagonizing her to complimenting her. Of course, she was instantly suspicious. *I need to ease into being friendlier. Water down my sincerity with some teasing until she trusts me more.*

"What a shame that is." I shake my head and make a tsking noise with my tongue. "I could be really good for you."

"Why do I find that hard to believe?" She scoffs with another eye roll, but she raises her eyebrows, waiting to see if I'll give her a reason.

"Because you're naturally suspicious?" I say innocently with a smile.

"More like I have hundreds of examples of you being a total shit-head to me."

"And I have just as many of you doing shit to piss me off."

"Well... you started it. You're a dick to me. I just match your energy."

Ouch. She's not wrong. I've always taken my frustration out on her. It's practically second nature now. I pull on the back of my neck to ease some of the nervous energy. *Here's my chance to turn this conversation around and I don't want to fuck it up.*

"That's fair." Her eyebrows shoot up as I meet her surprised gaze. "But you should know, I've regretted it every goddamn time."

Annie's glare intensifies as she narrows her eyes and studies my face, looking for signs of me bullshitting her. I hold eye contact with her, and the air around us crackles with tension.

"Annie! Did you still want to sing?" Leena's voice snaps us both out of our stare-down. We both blink as we find Leena watching us with an eyebrow quirked.

Annie recovers first, "Yeah. Um... do you have an acoustic I can borrow?"

Leena's eyebrows shoot up to her hairline. "Oh damn. Okay, let me have Cass get it tuned up."

"You play guitar?" I ask, the curiosity finally taking over. "I didn't know that."

"Well... I only know a handful of songs. Most of them by Saving Jane," she responds with a small smile. "That's why Leena was surprised. It's a truly shitty day when I'm busting out my comfort songs."

"Saving Jane? Dang, I forgot about them. They're from Ohio, right?"

"Yep! They were my absolute favorite when I was younger. I was obsessed with their first album. I'm still bummed that they didn't get more popular."

"I remember liking them," I say with a nod. I take a drink of my beer and glance back up to find Annie studying me again. "What?"

"That might be the most pleasant conversation we've ever had." She smirks as she takes a drink. "I didn't hate it."

"I told you I'm charming when you give me a chance." Giving her a cocky smile, something in her expression freezes a bit as she narrows her eyes. I'd pay a lot of money to read her mind right about now.

Leena comes back over with an acoustic guitar, and Annie makes her way up to the stage.

"Hey everyone, this is an older one, but one of my favorites for less than fantastic days and dealing with assholes. This is 'Reasons Why' by Saving Jane."

She launches into the upbeat song that is basically a screw you to anyone that's ever pissed her off. *Dammit.* I kind of thought we were making some progress here. I'm not sure if I'm included in the people she's telling off with the song lyrics, but I wouldn't be surprised.

I hate that she's having a shitty time, but I'm also completely entranced by her. Even if she is telling me to fuck off musically, I'm more determined than ever to get her to not completely despise me somehow.

A guy can dream, right?

MY PHONE RINGS WITH the FaceTime tone just as I walk in my front door. I peel off my winter coat, hat, and gloves, shaking off the snowflakes that coated them on my trip from the car to the door. I drop my keys into the little bowl on the table by the door and kick my shoes off. The phone stops ringing, but then immediately starts back up again as I'm pulling my phone from the pocket of my jeans.

My big sister Jenna is trying to FaceTime me. She likes to check in randomly, at least once a week. She's likely to keep calling until I answer. I smile as I plop onto my couch and answer the call.

"Hey, Jen Jen."

My sister's face fills my phone screen. We have the same blue eyes, but her hair is a brighter blonde than mine. It always was as kids, but I'm pretty sure it's salon-assisted these days. She has her hair braided in a long rope over her shoulder and is wearing one of my sweatshirts that she stole the last time she got chilly while hanging out here.

"Hi, Icky," she says with a grin. I roll my eyes at the nickname she insists on continuing to use. At least my childhood nickname for her isn't a damn insult.

"Whatcha doing? You're too dressed up to have spent your evening staring at your bookkeeping software." She smirks and squints at me through the phone. "Plus, your hair doesn't look like you've been trying to pull it all out."

"Hilarious," I deadpan back to her. It's a well-known fact in our family that I pull on my hair when I'm stressed. A nervous habit I've never been able to break. "I was out at an open mic night at my friend's bar."

"Oh yeah! Songbird! The girl dating Bailey owns it, right?"

"Yep, Leena."

"Is she one of the ones that's friends with—"

"Yes. She's friends with Annie."

"Of course, and what better way to get inside information about the secret love of your life?"

"Annie is not the love of my life. She's more like the bane of my existence. I can barely stand her."

Jenna rolls her eyes and scoffs. "You're either in a massive amount of denial or completely full of shit. I've been listening to you complain about Annie Martin for the last fifteen years. The sooner you realize you have feelings for this woman, the better off we all will be."

"First off, I've only known her for twelve years. Second, you've listened to me complain, because she's annoying and infuriating." I don't even know why I'm digging in on this, considering I know Jenna is more right than wrong on this one. The urge to argue with my sister is just too strong.

"Baby brother. I say this with love. Get a fucking grip. You like her, and for what it's worth, I'm pretty damn sure she likes you, too."

"Okay, now that's a stretch. There's no way she has any feelings for me besides loathing and contempt. Seriously, I tried to be nice to her tonight and she—"

"WAIT. She was actually there?"

Fuck. Now Jenna's never going to let me drop this topic. Not that she was likely to drop it in the first place. She's like a dog with a fucking bone when it comes to dissecting my love life.

"Her mom's having a knee replacement, so she's home for a while to help out."

"And you're her mom's PT, right?" she says, with a devious grin. "What an opportune time to spend a little time with Annie... Get a little closer."

"Jenna..."

"I'm just saying." The humor drops from her voice as she gets serious. "Listen, Eric. I'm worried about you. All you do is work, and I know you want a relationship, but you're not putting yourself out there to actually find one. Part of that is because you keep waiting for the same spark you feel with Annie. Maybe it's time to bury the hatchet, see if you two could become something more than mortal enemies."

I scoff a laugh. She had to go and get all sincere on me. "I could, maybe, admit to not hating Annie, but I don't think she'll ever feel the same way.

There's a lot of bad blood between us. Besides, I work all the time because I'm trying to save my practice from bankruptcy."

She winces, knowing all about my financial issues, but not being able to help with her degree in English Literature. She's just as bad with numbers as I am. "I'm sorry, Icky. Any more luck with figuring things out?"

"No, the new office manager I hired, Amber, doesn't seem to have any better of a grasp on what's going on than I do, even though she said she had bookkeeping experience. I ran into Fred Chambers tonight, and he's gonna come by and look at the books."

"Hopefully, he'll be able to help!" she says cheerfully before her face cracks into an enormous yawn. "Okay, well, I'm gonna go to bed. I stayed up way too late last night editing my work-in-progress before it goes to my editor next week."

My sister spent the last couple of years building a following as an indie romance author. I think she's on book six or seven, and as far as I know, she's killing it. She even quit her admin job to write full-time this fall.

"Okay, Jen Jen. Get some rest."

"You too, Icky. And... think about what I said. About Annie."

I nod and end the call. I shake my head and heave myself off the couch to get ready for bed. As if I can think about anything but Annie. Even when I was sure I hated her, she occupied my thoughts more often than not.

Now, when I know Jenna is probably spot on, with her theories, getting Annie out of my head would take a goddamn miracle.

Chapter Five

Annie

I'M MILDLY HUNGOVER WHEN I meet Leena and Jessie for breakfast the next day at The Main Bite, Fort Starling's fifties-style diner, complete with checkerboard floor and jukebox. Those last couple of beers I had last night were a bad idea, but the shit-tastic day combined with Eric being super weird made them feel necessary.

I collapse into the booth across from the one Leena and Jessie are occupying while they study the breakfast menu. Leena's eyebrows shoot up as she eyes me.

"You good, A.?" Jessie asks, concerned. I must look worse than I thought.

"Yeah, a little hungover. Plus, I didn't sleep well."

"That have anything to do with you and Eric chit-chatting last night? You almost looked friendly."

I roll my eyes. Hard. "One non-hostile conversation does not make us friends. If anything, it weirded me out."

They share a long look, and I shake my head at them. One semi-nice interaction does not make Eric and me any less than enemies, and they need to get any other ideas out of their heads.

"I had too many drinks thanks to my career imploding spectacularly, thank you very much."

Leena winces and shoots me an apologetic glance.

"I don't get why this douchebag has it out for you? I mean, it's one thing to give new clients to his girlfriend, but why is he trying to fuck you over?" Jessie asks.

I cringe and hold my hand over my eyes. "I may not have told you guys the entire story." Both sets of eyebrows shoot up as they wait for me to fill them in. "Ugh! I kinda sort of had a fling with Kevin first, at the beginning of the year. I got ahead of myself thinking we were gonna be a thing, and he ghosted me. News flash, Kevin, you can't ghost someone you work with seventy hours a week."

"That bastard." Leena practically growls.

"Right. We still worked together, and he was onto asking Serena out the next week."

They both make sounds of outrage.

"Exactly. So, I called him out on it. But... I may have done it in the office with lots of people around to overhear... how I faked it with him because he was boring in bed."

"Oh Annie, no." Jessie murmurs.

"Yep. Lost my temper big time."

"Were you faking it?" Leena asks with a smirk.

"Yeah. I mean, it wasn't terrible, but he didn't really try all that hard. I got so caught up in the vision of us being this power couple that I figured I could overlook it. Which I know sounds totally pathetic."

I slump down in my seat, feeling like the world's biggest loser. It's my own stupid fault, too. I knew better than to sleep with my boss. I tried so hard to resist his tall, dark, and handsome gimmick. The unrelenting crush

I kept to myself for months, never letting on that I was daydreaming about us being the next power couple at the firm.

When he finally asked me out, I was thrilled. I could see the future unfurling in front of me. Sure, the sex was boring, and we had nothing to talk about other than work, but this was the dream. We'd take the Chicago financial scene by storm as partners both in the office and at home.

Then he was done with me and onto asking Serena to dinner. Serena was quick to rub it in my face that he chose her over me. Even now, almost a year later, I can't help but wonder what it is about me that makes me not worth the effort. So easy to leave behind.

"Why didn't you tell us any of this?" Leena asks kindly, but she also sounds hurt that I kept something this big from them.

"Well, it all went down when you and Bailey were in the early stages of your whole thing, so I didn't want to get into it." I let out a big sigh and shrug. "And I was embarrassed. I mean, I got overly attached to an asshole who also happens to be my boss and harpooned my career."

"He was definitely partially responsible. The whole giving your clients away because you embarrassed him is plain wrong," Jessie says as she grabs my hand across the table.

"Yeah. This whole thing screams sexual harassment. He used his position to get you into bed, and now he's retaliating at you for calling him out," Leena adds.

"Could you file a complaint?" Jessie asks.

I shrug my shoulders and let out another enormous sigh as my eyes fill with tears. After keeping all this to myself for so long, it feels wonderful to have my friends' support.

"I kind of want to be done with it. I don't know. Part of me wants to quit and move home, but then part of me wants to claw my way back up. Leaving Chicago and coming home feels like I've failed."

"I think you have to decide what will make you happy. Are you happy in Chicago?" Leena asks with raised eyebrows as if she already knows the answer and just wants to make me say it out loud.

"Not lately," I admit. "But I still feel like I could be."

"Okay, then you keep it on the table and make the most of the situation right now. What are you going to do for three months?" Jessie interjects, patting my hand.

"I'm gonna move into the apartment over the Songbird—thanks again, Leens—and I guess find a short-term accounting gig? I don't know who's hiring right now with Christmas so close, though."

We all go quiet for a moment, racking our brains for businesses that would need accounting help three weeks before Christmas. I guess the temporary job hunt could wait until after New Year's, but I don't love the idea of waiting that long to get it settled.

"Oh, hey! There's Fred! Let's ask him!" Leena waves to the older man who is standing at the counter waiting for a to-go order. He gives us a big smile and comes over to our booth.

Fred has been a surrogate grandpa to all of us over the years. He and his wife, Gail, were good friends with Leena's Gram, so they were all around while we were growing up. They usually made an appearance during our holiday gatherings. I don't know what Christmas will look like this year, with Mom's surgery.

"Well, if it isn't some of my favorite ladies! How you doing this morning?" Fred booms out. We all murmur our hellos as he smiles at us.

"Fred, Annie's looking for some accounting work while she's in town for a few months. Have you heard of anyone hiring right now?" Leena asks.

"Hmm. Can't say I know of anyone off the top of my head, but I'll keep my ear to the ground and ask around for you, Annie Lou."

"Thanks, Fred." I give the man a big smile, wishing he still had his accounting firm going. I'd go to work for him in a heartbeat. The waitress at the counter calls Fred's name for his order.

"Looks like my order is ready and Gail's waiting. I'll see you girls later!"

He grabs the bag from the waitress and takes off out the front of the diner.

"That man is a treasure," I murmur as we watch him leave to take breakfast to his wife of fifty-plus years. "You guys are lucky you've found your other halves. It's rough out there."

When I glance up at them, they're both giving me radiant smiles, but only Leena's meets her eyes. There's something off about Jessie's expression. Before I can ask her about it, our food shows up. I make a mental note to check in with her soon as I dig into my strawberry-banana French toast.

"You'll find your person. He's out there somewhere," Jessie insists as she tucks into her eggs.

"Yeah, well, I know one thing. I'm never sleeping with anyone who can make my life hell at work again. Bosses are completely off-limits."

"A boss boycott?" Leena snarks as she holds up a slice of bacon.

"Exactly!" I agree with a nod. "I've learned my lesson for sure."

"Mom?" I call out as I stomp the snow from my boots on the mat we have at the kitchen door when I get home from breakfast.

"We're in here, Annie!" she calls from the living room at the front of the house.

We? I come to a sharp stop at the entrance as I see who her visitor is. Mom is sitting on the couch with her leg up, an ice pack resting across her knee, and Eric is sitting in the armchair sorting through paperwork that he hands to her.

"You remember Dr. Reynolds, right, dear?" Mom says it with a smile, but her voice is tight with a hidden warning to be nice. She remembers exactly how unpleasantly I behaved around Eric last spring.

"Ah. What a lovely surprise," I deadpan in the most sarcastic tone of voice I can manage. I don't care if Mom thinks I'm being a brat. I've learned to be on the offensive with Eric at all times.

"Hi, Annie," Eric says and gives me a kind smile. "It's good to see you."

"Okay, who are you and what have you done with Eric, the asshole?" He's being nice and normal, and it instantly has me on alert. Is he just trying to lower my defenses so he can go in for the kill with something scathing and hurtful? Lord knows, this man loves to hurt my feelings, not that I'd admit to him that he's ever succeeded.

"Annie! Behave, please," my mom exclaims exasperatedly.

"Don't worry about it, Sherrie. Annie has plenty of reasons to be suspicious."

I'm preparing myself to trade insults, but that response pulls me up short. What the fuck is going on with him? Where's the cutting insult?

"Right. I do. Because, usually, you can't resist saying something hateful."

"Yeah, I'm working on that." He shoots me a smirk as he puts the paperwork my mom handed him back into his folder and stands. "Although I could argue I'm usually provoked."

He raises his eyebrows in challenge. Literally provoking me while he tries to claim that I'm the one who starts shit. I, of course, rise to the challenge since I can't seem to control my temper with this man.

"I don't provoke you! You always start it."

"Are you sure? I'm pretty sure I was nice to you at the bar the other night." He crosses his arms over his chest, and I swear he does it just so that his biceps seem extra massive. He quirks an eyebrow at me. He's baiting me, but that doesn't stop me from crossing my own arms and stepping directly in front of him. I totally don't notice how much I like that I have to crane my neck to gaze up at him. Nope, I don't notice that at all.

"Oh, right. I'm so sorry. Of course, one non-hostile conversation out of hundreds of interactions clearly erases all the times you've been a total jerk," I snark back. Since I'm holding his gaze, I don't miss the wince and the flash of something that looks suspiciously like regret that crosses his expression.

Huh, that's new.

"You're right." His tone is so sincere that I'm struck completely dumb. My arms drop to my sides, and I stand blinking up into his blue eyes. He reaches out and tucks a loose lock of hair behind my ear, making my breath stutter. "And I'm sorry."

We stare at each other for a few heartbeats before he takes a deep breath and steps back, breaking eye contact. My mom sits on the couch studying us intently, and Eric clears his throat before grabbing his bag.

"Sherrie, I'll be back once you're home from the hospital. Just have Annie give my office a call once you have your discharge date, and we'll get your PT going."

"Thank you, Eric. We'll see you next week."

He gives us both a smile and a nod and leaves through the front door. I'm still standing frozen until the door clicks shut. I collapse into the armchair he was sitting in when I entered the room. The scent of his cologne lingers in the air, and I can't resist taking a deep inhale.

"I have no idea what just happened," I say, stunned.

Mom smirks at me. "I don't know either, but I could see the sparks from here."

"It's not like that with Eric. We hate each other," I say, but all the venom has completely evaporated. Mom just hums in response. "What?"

"I know you have a complicated history with Eric, but I don't think either of you hates the other. In fact, I'd be willing to bet you actually like each other very much."

I huff out a humorless laugh. "That's crazy, Mom. I do not like Eric. And I don't trust this nice guy act he's trying to pull."

"What if he's actually a nice guy?"

"I don't buy it. He's up to something. Plus, he's a man, so there's already a reason not to trust him."

Mom shakes her head and furrows her brow as she studies me for a moment. "When did you become so cynical, Annie Lou?"

"Mama, I have literally never met a man who hasn't let me down. Except for Fred Chambers, of course, but I'm not sure he counts because the man's practically a saint. Every other man I've ever known has either hurt me or left me, so why should I trust any of them?"

Mom purses her lips and stays quiet for a long moment, thinking over my question. "I hate that for you. I know your father did some damage, leaving the way he did when you were so young. But if you look around, you'll find some other trustworthy men in your life besides Fred. Dan? Leena's boyfriend? Do you trust them with your friends' hearts and well-being?"

"Well, yeah, but—"

"That means trustworthy men exist. You have to keep your heart open, Annie Lou. Closing it off is never the answer."

"I get what you're saying. But that doesn't mean I can trust Eric. He's given me lots of reasons not to."

"How many of those are from when he was a dumb eighteen-year-old kid?"

Shit. This is why Mom is such an excellent lawyer. It's infuriating that I can never win an argument with her, but it also low-key makes me proud knowing she's so good at her job.

"Fair point. Most of them."

"Then I guess you should give him a chance to show you who he is now. I think he's already started doing that."

I blink at Mom for a second before she shoots me the same smile she always wears when she knows she's won. I grumble something about taking a nap and escape the room.

I shake my head to clear the after-effects of both the conversation with Mom and Eric's strange, nice guy transformation. I'm sure it was just a weird interaction. He'll be back to being a dirtbag the next time I see him.

Unless... Could I have been wrong about him all along?

Chapter Six

Eric

"WHAT DO YOU MEAN, the numbers aren't adding up?" Practically growling into the phone, I interrupt my latest office manager's rambling. I'm so frustrated, I could scream. It doesn't help that I was already keyed up from Annie calling me out on my dickish behavior, and now my office manager can't seem to figure out what's going on with the practice's books any more than I can. I run my hand through my hair and give it a yank, trying to calm my temper. "What isn't adding up, Amber?"

"I'm not really sure," Amber mumbles into the phone. "I keep re-balancing the accounts receivable ledger, but it's not lining up with the payments. This is, um... a bit more complicated than anything I've done before."

"You said you have bookkeeping experience. It was on your resume," I clip out through gritted teeth.

"Well... I do, but it wasn't like this." The whine in her voice grates on my nerves.

"I'll figure it out when I get back to the office," I snap. "I just got to the Flash stadium, so I'll be back after their appointments. Probably around three."

Hanging up the phone before she can start whining about something else, I close my eyes and take a deep breath. This isn't really Amber's fault and I definitely owe her an apology for taking my frustration out on her.

I hired her about a month ago, and while she's an excellent office manager, great with the patients, and keeps the office running smoothly, it's clear that my bookkeeping mess is more challenging than she can handle. I'll see what ideas Fred has for fixing the disaster of my books on Friday.

I do my best to shake off my frustration with Amber and the accounts as I head into the Flash stadium. As one of the smaller teams in the major league, they only have a couple of part-time trainers on staff, so I've been doing PT with some players on the roster. Mostly the guys I'm friends with, like Bailey and Dan Chase, my buddy from college.

"Hey, Doc! My shoulder's being a little bitch again. I thought you fixed it," Dan yells out across the weight room when I walk in.

"Are you doing the exercises I taught you?" I raise my eyebrows and fix him with a mock-serious glare.

"Yeah, mostly," he mumbles back, suddenly sheepish.

"Let's go, Chase. You can be first up."

Bailey snickers at him and gives me a wave. He follows us to the training room. "Doc, what's going on with your hair? You look like you got electrocuted."

I run my hand through my hair, smoothing down the mess I made of it while talking to Amber. "Oh, just a frustrating conversation with my office manager. If I don't find someone to fix the practice's financials soon, I'm going to be bald."

"Damn. I thought you liked this one? Amy?"

"Amber. She's a decent enough office manager, but it's clear she doesn't have the bookkeeping skills I need. I'm gonna have to hire an accountant or something. Fred Chambers is stopping by Friday to take a look at everything and give me suggestions."

"That's good. He should be able to help," Bailey says. He and Dan share a pointed glance, having a telepathic conversation.

"Something you two want to share with the class? You're like an old married couple having a silent argument." I roll my eyes in their direction and give my head a shake as I move to help Dan stretch out his shoulder.

"Just... you know, Annie. She's pretty much an accounting genius. And she's looking for a job." Dan clears his throat. "Might be an option for you?"

Fuck. Annie is everywhere today. My pulse takes off just at the mention of her. I need to get my shit together.

"Annie Martin?" I scoff. "Why is she looking for a job here? I thought she'd go back to Chicago after her mom's surgery."

They share another cagey look before Bailey clears his throat. "She's, uh, had a bit of a rough time of it. Looks like she'll be here for at least the next few months, maybe longer."

"What happened?"

"Listen, man, the girls said we weren't really supposed to talk about it... It seems Annie was pretty embarrassed, but I guess she's had some problems with her boss being an asshole." Dan tugs at the back of his neck and avoids eye contact. They clearly know more than they're willing to share, likely sworn to secrecy by their significant others.

My heart squeezes in my chest. I hate the idea of Annie struggling. It's one thing to give her a hard time myself, but the idea of her boss treating her badly sparks a protective fire that catches me off guard. I swallow hard to tamp down the rage that's suddenly threatening to take over.

"You realize she hates me, right? We can't have a civil conversation without fighting. How would working together be a good idea?" I ask incredulously.

"I wouldn't be so sure. You guys seemed to have a decent conversation at the bar last night," Bailey interjects.

"Plus, don't forget how you pined after her your entire freshman year," Dan adds with a smirk. "You picked fights because you *like* her."

I roll my eyes hard at Dan's singsongy bullshit. "Fuck off, I did not. I picked fights because she's obnoxious."

"Dude, you're forgetting I was there the night you met. You were a smitten kitten, for sure." Dan waggles his eyebrows at me; the temptation to throat punch him dances through my brain.

"How would you know? You were too busy studying Jessie's tonsils to pay any attention to anything back then."

"Ah, the good old days." Dan sighs. He's joking around, but there's an edge to his tone that makes me wonder if there may be trouble in paradise for him and Jessie. I'm about to ask about it when Bailey interjects.

"Regardless of how you felt about her when you were in college, she could be just what you need now. What your business needs."

"I'll consider it. Now start doing your knee exercises or I'm gonna be here with you assholes all day."

Bailey shoots me a grin and starts in on his reps to strengthen his knee that's been acting up. With Dan and Bailey distracted by their exercises, I let my mind wander back to Annie.

Our sparring earlier today felt less hateful than in the past, and she looked genuinely surprised when I apologized. Dan isn't that far off base with what he said about freshman year. I can try to deny it, but I down bad for her back then. What would working with her every day be like now?

The way that idea warms my blood makes me think it's probably not a good plan, but I'm not sure if I can resist helping her out. If she needs a job, any help really, I want to be the one to be there for her.

Shit. I'm in trouble.

"YOU'VE GOT QUITE A mess here, son." Fred gives me a sympathetic pat on the arm as he confirms what I already knew. "You're gonna need to hire a consultant to go back through your records to see where things went wrong and get everything tidied back up. This looks like it is not a new situation. I'm seeing issues and discrepancies going back months."

"Yeah. It's more likely years." I drag my hands through my hair.

"What the hell happened, if you don't mind my asking?"

"I trusted my first office manager to take care of everything. She'd print me off reports, and everything looked good on the surface, so I just rolled with it. I trusted she had everything right. Then she retired and moved to Florida, and I found out the accounts were a mess. I haven't been able to fix it myself, and the three office managers I've gone through in the meantime only made the mess worse."

"You're gonna need some serious help here," he says as he flips through the reports I printed out. "Even if I were still working, this would be a bit of a puzzle for me to work out. You're gonna need someone who knows their stuff."

"Do you have anyone in mind?"

"You happen to know Annie Martin?" Fred asks with a squint. "You're friends with Leena and her crew, right?"

I let out a big breath. "Yeah. I know Annie. We went to college together. We...um... haven't always gotten along."

Fred nods his head and studies the reports a bit more. "Well, whatever happened in the past, I figure she's the one you want digging into this. She's got the math brain and the audit experience you'll need for cleaning up this mess. Plus, she's looking for a temporary job. It would work out perfectly for both of you."

Yeah, if we can keep from murdering each other. I keep that thought to myself as I thank Fred for his time.

"I really appreciate you coming over, Mr. Chambers."

"Son, you're in your thirties. Call me Fred." He shoots me a big grin as he pulls his coat back on and pauses at my office door. "You'll think about reaching out to Annie? I'm telling you, she's the one."

His phrasing hits me like a bullet to the chest. *The one.* For a moment, I'm transported back to that autumn day when I first met Annie at a fraternity party. She was stunning, smart, and funny. I had never met a girl that I so completely connected with before, and I was instantly obsessed with her. We talked for hours, but when I popped into the bathroom for a minute, she disappeared.

My roommate told me she had to leave with her friend. Leena and Jessie were both at the party with her, so I figured one of them needed to leave. I understood, but I was disappointed to have missed my chance to ask her out. Or at least get her number.

I searched fraternity parties, every corner of campus, for two months before I found her in my room. As my roommate's girlfriend. Pretty sure I stopped believing in "the one" right then and there.

Annie may not be my "one" in the romantic sense, but it's pretty clear that she's the person I need to help save my practice. That is, if I can convince her to come work for me.

Fuck, I'm in so much trouble.

"Ah! It's happening!" Jenna practically squeals as she dances in her seat. "I knew you were gonna get together!"

"Jenna. How the fuck did you get that out of 'I need to ask Annie to come work for me?' And lower your voice. Everyone's staring."

My gruff tone does nothing to dissuade Jenna from shimmying her shoulders in her seat. I pinch the bridge of my nose, already regretting meeting her for dinner. But we finally got a Piada in Fort Starling and my sister is obsessed. It's one of her favorite restaurants to get when we're in Columbus, so she was pumped that we were getting one in town. Plus, you can't go wrong with a build-your-own pasta bowl when you're attempting to eat your anxiety.

"You're going to be with each other all the time. All that sexual tension in a tiny office space. There's no way you guys won't crack and end up doing it on your desk."

"Jen Jen. Please don't talk to me about doing it. I literally can't have this conversation with you."

She rolls her eyes at me. Jenna is a chronic over-sharer with the details of her sex life, despite her knowing it makes me uncomfortable.

She waves me off with a flick of her wrist, "Don't be a prude, Icky! So, how did you leave it the last time you saw her?"

"Uh, okay, I think. Apologized for acting like a dick in the past. I think she could tell I meant it... I mean, I hope she could tell. I don't know. She was definitely weirded out that I was trying to be nice, which makes me feel even worse for all the times I was an asshole to her."

"Yeah, not your best move, Icky. Why have you been such a dick to her all these years?"

"Well, it started because she dated my roommate. I was butthurt she blew me off for him and lashed out."

"Seems like a gross overreaction," she mumbles through a bite of pasta.

"It was just after all that drama happened with Steve..." I let my voice trail off.

"Ah. Well, that makes more sense. You were eighteen and dealing with some bullshit. Although, to be fair to my future sister-in-law, you could have stopped being a dick sooner."

"Jenna, you have got to stop thinking about Annie like that. She barely tolerates me. Future sister-in-law is not a possibility. At this point, I'm hoping for 'friendly acquaintance that will help me bail out my business'."

"Fine. You can start there. But I'm telling you, I'm right about this one."

"Whatever you say, Jen Jen."

I roll my eyes at her and focus on eating, but her words are lodged in my brain. She's right, I could have stopped being a dick to Annie sooner. We've run into each other every couple of years, mostly thanks to Dan and Jessie.

Every time, it turned into a fight. What makes me think we can get along now?

Still, I have to try. To save my business, but also to quiet the part of my brain that is always asking, what if?

What if I'd gotten Annie's number that night? What if we ran into each other on campus sooner? What if we'd dated? What if we fell in love?

What if it's not too late?

Chapter Seven

Annie

"I'M GONNA GRAB A shower real quick. What time did Eric's office say he'd be here?" I call out to Mom from the kitchen as I'm filling her ice pack. I grab her water bottle and the sandwich I made her for lunch.

Mom is reclining on the couch with her knee propped up on pillows. Her expression is full of exhaustion and pain. Knee replacements are fucking intense, and it seems this one is a little worse than last time. Her good knee is still healing from the surgery last May, so it's no wonder she's struggling.

I glance at my watch to see that it's almost noon, confirming that it's about time for her next dose of meds. Excellent timing, since she'll want those in her system if she's going to be doing physical therapy.

"Um... the receptionist said he'd be here around one-thirty," Mom answers in a groggy voice.

"Perfect. You can take your painkillers with lunch and still have a little time for a nap before PT."

Mom responds with something that sounds like a grunt mixed with a hum. Even four days post-surgery, she's still in pretty rough shape. They kept her at the hospital for the first two days, and she came home yesterday, but I know it's hard for her to rest while she's in so much pain.

"Need anything else before I get in the shower?"

She shakes her head no, and I dash up the stairs to my bathroom. While the shower heats, I lay out my clothes for the day. I grab my comfy boyfriend jeans, then waver between two different tops, wanting to look cute but not like I'm trying too hard.

Shit. Since when do I care what Eric thinks? We hate each other.

Even in my head, the thought doesn't quite ring true anymore. I'm thinking it never really did, at least on my end. I step into the hot steam as I let my mind wander back to college.

I can still remember the moment I saw Eric across the dingy party house basement. Our eyes met, and our gazes locked for what felt like forever. Time stopped, and the party around us disappeared for an instant. When we got to talking later on, we clicked right away, chatting about *The Office,* movie musicals, and how disgusting we both thought avocados were.

I would have gone home with him in a heartbeat. Hookups have never really been my style, even back then, but there was something about him. Unfortunately, Leena chose the moment he stepped away to the bathroom to reappear, drunk off her ass and on the verge of getting sick. We had to get her out of there, so I quickly scribbled my number on a scrap of paper and left it with Eric's roommate, Scott. Eric never used it.

My feelings were bruised, but the attraction to Eric never quite went away, even when I was dating Scott. The constant sparring with Eric every time we were in the same room was such a turn-on. The sparks between us lit me up every time we fought.

They still do, if I'm being honest with myself.

I pause, doing mental math of how long it will take me to get ready before I grab the hand-held shower head. I have time, and if I'm going to deal with Eric, I'd rather be relaxed going into it.

I turn the knob on the showerhead to switch the pressure to a concentrated stream. It almost stings my skin with its strength. The water stream roams over my nipples before I travel it down across my belly. I lean my weight against the wall of the shower, the cold tile a sharp contrast to the steam filling the small room and the heat racing through my body. I lean my head back and close my eyes as the warm water travels lower and lower.

I position myself low against the wall, spreading my legs wide and moving the showerhead lower so that the strong jet of water is aimed right at my clit. The strength of the water hitting that sensitive bundle of nerves has my legs shaking in seconds.

I move the showerhead in tight circles, giving my clit pulsing waves of water pressure, and moving one finger to my entrance. I suddenly regret not grabbing my waterproof vibrator before hopping in the shower, but I make do with my hand and the showerhead.

I refocus the stream of water on my clit and hold it there. I squeeze my eyes tight as the pressure takes over and my upper body curls in on itself. It doesn't take long before an intense orgasm has me clenching every muscle in my body as the waves roll over me.

I catch my breath, leaning against the wall of the shower, moving the showerhead back to its normal pressure setting. Once my heart rate returns to a semi-normal rate, I stand back up and finish washing quickly.

It's only as I'm pulling my clothes on that I realize I pictured Eric's strong hands on my body and his sparkling blue eyes when I came.

"THAT'S IT, SHERRIE, JUST a few more steps." Eric's smooth voice echoes from the front hall, where Mom shuffles slowly with a walker as Eric walks backwards in front of her. "Okay, let's turn around and go back. That's it; take your time."

I squeeze my thighs together as I listen to his kind encouragement. Apparently, Eric being sweet to my mother is even more of a turn-on than him fighting with me. He's a great physical therapist, and he's been on his best behavior the whole time he's been here. It's totally weird, but also kind of nice. My mind, and body for that matter, are confused about how we're supposed to feel about Eric.

When Mom reaches the couch, we both help her get situated with her leg propped up, and Eric places the icepack across the top of her knee. He jots down a few notes and puts his iPad back in his messenger bag. He straightens up to leave, but pauses and looks at me, clearing his throat.

"Annie, could I talk to you for a minute?"

My eyebrows rise at his polite tone, but I follow him to the front door, intrigued. Standing in the tiny hallway, I'm hit with the scent of whatever cologne he uses, and I have to squeeze my thighs together all over again. He smells so good, I have to bite the inside of my cheek to keep from burying my nose in his chest.

"What's up?" I say, more sharply than necessary.

"Um... the guys and Fred Chambers all mentioned that you were looking for a job?" He tugs at the back of his neck like he's nervous.

"Yeah, something temporary. I'll be here for a few months. I'm gonna move into the apartment over the Songbird once Mom's back on her feet."

He nods, and I raise my eyebrows again, waiting for him to continue.

"Well... uh... I need help. Accounting help. Fred thought you might be the right person." I don't speak for a moment, shocked that Eric is asking me for help. Offering me a job right when I need it. I'm almost suspicious that he's up to something shitty, or playing a mean joke but then he meets my eyes, and I see the desperation in them.

I blow out a shaky breath. "What do you need help with? Also, we usually can't be in the same room without fighting. Do you really think me working for you would be a good idea?"

"The practice books are a mess. Fred said it was like a puzzle and that you'd be the best person for the job." He runs his hand through his hair and blows out a shaky breath. "Annie, I'm trying...I'm trying to be on my best behavior here. I know I haven't always treated you well, and I'm sorry for that. I don't want to be that guy anymore. And... I need you."

The pleading tone of his speech, mixed with the blazing sincerity shining out of his crystal blue eyes knocks the wind out of me for a moment. I swallow hard and study him for a long beat. What Mom said about giving him a chance to show me who he is now echoes in my head.

"Fine. But if asshole Eric makes a reappearance, I'm gone," I say, crossing my arms over my chest.

"I mean. I'm gonna try, but you tend to bring him out more than anyone else." He shoots me the cocky smirk I'm used to, but it's changed somehow. It's like he's traded out the asshole for this flirty guy and it makes my temperature spike. I just agreed to work for this man. I cannot be flirting with him.

"Okay. Tomorrow morning, I'll come by to figure out what we're working with. We can discuss rates then. I want to know what I'm getting into before I decide how much it's gonna cost you." I raise my eyebrows, waiting for him to argue. He only nods. He must really need help with those books. "I can only do a couple of hours a day until Mom is more mobile, but after that, I'm all yours."

For just a second, his eyes darken as a spark of heat crosses his expression. It's gone before I can be sure it was there, but my heart rate is already all over the place.

"Thank you, Annie. I really, really appreciate it." His gaze continues to hold mine until I nod and look away, breaking the thread that's formed between us.

"See you in the morning, Boss Man."

He shakes his head and huffs out a laugh. "See ya, sweetheart."

I exaggeratedly roll my eyes at him and cross my arms, if only to cover the visceral reaction my body is having to him.

"I already regret this. And I'm not your sweetheart."

He laughs as he walks to his car, and I close the door behind him. I lean against the door to take a moment to get a fucking grip. Not easy, considering his delicious scent is lingering in the small entryway. I have years of evidence of Eric being an asshole. Just because he's been nicer lately does not give me permission to get all swoony over him.

Besides, he's going to be my boss now, and I meant what I told the girls at breakfast the other day. There's no way I'm getting involved with another boss. The boss boycott is on, and I'm not making the same mistake again.

Eric is officially off-limits.

THE NEXT MORNING, I get to Eric's office right at opening time. The practice sits in the corner unit of a newer strip mall with a few other random businesses. I'm instantly excited to discover a BIGGBY Coffee drive-through that shares the same parking lot. I'll be upping my coffee budget while I'm working here because I cannot resist getting regular Scuba Blasts and Butter Bear Lattes.

Not knowing what to wear, I mixed casual and professional styles when I got ready this morning. I landed on a hot pink blazer with a lighter pink silk tank, my favorite skinny jeans, and ankle booties. I threw my good wool coat over the top for a layer of warmth, thanks to the frigid December temperatures.

When I enter the office, I find the receptionist is wearing sporty joggers and a polo with a Reynolds PT logo, so I'm instantly glad I didn't go with full office wear. The office is cozy and warm inside, with the scents of cinnamon and vanilla in the air to match the Christmas decorations covering the front desk area.

I smile at the girl at the front desk and offer her my hand. "Hi, I'm Annie. I'm here to help with the accounting?"

She looks like she's in her early twenties, probably fresh out of college. She has dark brown hair, almost black, that is pulled into a smart ponytail.

Her big, dark eyes take me in as she gives me a wobbly, timid smile back. "I'm Amber. I'm the office manager... for now, anyway."

"Oh, are you planning on leaving? Are you in school or something?" I furrow my brow as her eyes fill with tears.

"No. I just know I messed up the accounts. I think Dr. Reynolds might let me go," she practically whispers to me.

I have no idea why this girl is confiding in me in the first thirty seconds of being in the building, but I already like her. I squeeze her arm and give her a warm smile.

"You leave Dr. Reynolds to me," I say with a wink. "Why don't you point me to his office?"

The main area of the office is a wide-open room. A variety of exercise equipment and massage-type tables fill the room. Amber gives me directions to follow the back hallway to the last door on the left to find Eric's office.

I give the door a sharp knock, and I hear Eric's deep voice letting me know to come in. I open the door to see him sitting at a large wooden U-shaped desk that takes up most of the room. There's a desktop computer in the back corner of the desk with a pile of files sitting in front of it. A comfy-looking desk chair waits, tucked in under the desk.

Eric is sitting on the outside of the desk in a smaller desk chair, staring at his laptop's screen. His brow is furrowed as he glares at his computer screen, so focused that he doesn't look up right away, giving me a moment to study him.

His dark blonde hair is spiked in random directions, making it clear he's been pulling on it. It must be an anxious habit of his because I definitely saw him do that the other day. The same cologne from the other day fills the small space. I swallow hard before clearing my throat.

"You know you're usually supposed to sit on the other side of the desk, right?" I ask, crossing my arms and leaning on the door frame casually.

Eric's eyes snap up to mine, and he gives me a smile that makes my heart skip a beat. *Off-limits*, I mentally remind myself.

"I figured it would be better if you used the big computer and desk, since most of the records are on it. I use the laptop more, so I can hang out on this side."

"So we'll be sharing this office? Sure, we couldn't have a civil conversation until last week, but yeah, it's a great idea for us to share a small, enclosed space. We totally won't kill each other," I deadpan.

"Exactly." He smirks up at me, ignoring my sarcasm. "I'm not in the office all that much since I'd rather be out on the floor. I usually only spend time here when I'm trying to struggle through understanding the books, and that's what you're here for. It'll be fine."

I roll my eyes and shake my head at him as I set my bag down. Pulling out the chair, I turn it so I'm facing him. I pull a fresh notebook and my own laptop out of my bag. I uncap my pen and look up at Eric, who's been watching me.

"Okay, walk me through what's going on with your books."

He clears his throat softly and shakes his head. "Um, well... I had an office manager who I thought had everything under control. I dropped the ball and didn't really pay attention to things under the surface. So when she retired about eight months ago, I discovered how much of a mess everything was."

He runs his hair through his hair, and I press my lips into a firm line to not smile at the gesture. I'm enjoying seeing this real, vulnerable version of Eric way more than I should be.

"I've hired a couple more office managers in the last few months, but they only made it worse, and I haven't been able to fix things," he finishes, blowing out a puff of air.

I nod my head as I take some notes. "Do you know where things went wrong? Also, do you think that the first office manager was skimming?"

"No... but honestly, I don't know for sure. Umm... numbers *really* aren't my strong suit, so it all blurs together after a bit. I thought I could trust Vicki, but..."

He tugs at the back of his neck as he trails off; he's clearly embarrassed that he's struggling with this side of his business. Against my better judgment, I reach my hand across the desk to pat the hand he has resting on the surface. I do my best to ignore the sparks shooting up my arm at the contact and smile at him.

"We'll get it figured out."

"You were right," he says with his eyebrows raised.

"About what?"

The cocky smirk makes its return. "It's fucking weird having you be nice to me. I get it now why it threw you off so much the other night."

I let out a loud laugh at that, and his smirk turns into a genuine smile. I shake my head at him.

"Well, don't get used to it," I snark back at him. "Now, tell me about Amber. Are you planning on firing her? Because there is no fucking way someone with a typical admin level of accounting experience could figure all of this out."

His eyebrows shoot up with surprise at my sudden rant. He holds his hands up in surrender. "I'm not planning on firing Amber. Where'd you get that?"

"The poor girl was practically in tears at the front desk when I told her I was here to work on the books. She thinks you're going to let her go."

"She said that?" he asks quietly, instantly chagrined. He pulls on his hair again, and once again, I press my lips together to stop myself from smiling. I don't know why I'm finding it so endearing. "Shit. I'll talk to her. I might have taken some of my frustration with the bookkeeping out on her."

"You'll talk to her and..." I raise my eyebrows and wait.

"And... I'll get her an apology BIGGBY gift card. Better?"

"Better." I nod with a smirk and turn towards the desktop computer. "Okay. Let's fire up this bad boy and see what we're working with."

Chapter Eight

Eric

I'VE ALWAYS BEEN ATTRACTED to Annie, but after the last hour of watching her, I'm in awe and a little bit hard. She's sorted through the files and records that looked like utter gibberish to me, like they're the simplest thing. She's made notes, started a spreadsheet, and has already untangled some things. Competence porn is a real thing.

"Okay. I've got a grasp on how bad things are," she finally says. She scribbles something at the bottom of the notebook and turns it towards me. "That's how much you'll need to pay me to fix it."

My eyes bulge out of my head at the number. "What is this? A week? Annie, you were just looking at my books. I can't afford this."

She chuckles at my panic. "No, Eric. That's a flat consulting fee to get everything worked out and fixed. It'll probably take me close to the full three months of leave that I'm on to get it all taken care of. So, divide that by twelve and you have the weekly if you want to break it down."

"Christ. You almost gave me a heart attack. That's doable," I say weakly, the tension draining out of my muscles with relief. "What about after those three months?"

"I'm hoping to be back in Chicago by then," she says with a cringe I can't quite decipher. "I can help you find someone to help with the book-keeping once we get things straightened out. I could even train Amber so she can add that back into her job duties once it's not a giant clusterfuck anymore."

My heart sinks a bit at the thought of her going back to Chicago. I need to keep my feelings for Annie in check. She's only here temporarily.

"I can't thank you enough for stepping in here, Annie."

"Eric, you're paying me. It's not like I'm doing you a favor." She shrugs and doesn't meet my eyes as she packs up her belongings. I don't want her to leave yet, but I know she needs to go home to check in on Sherrie.

"Pretty sure forgiving me for being such an asshole to you in the past is doing me a big favor." I give her my usual smirk and meet her eyes. I can't resist teasing her as I meet her near the door.

"Who says I forgave you? What's that saying about keeping your enemies close?"

She crosses her arms and tries to glare at me, but I can see the humor sparkling in her expression, her brown eyes reminding me of warm caramel syrup. I purposely take a step closer to her so she has to tilt her face up to look at me. She goes still as I invade her space a bit; the only movement is her breathing picking up pace, like she's out of breath.

"Enemies, huh? Isn't there also a saying about love and hate being two sides of the same coin?"

"I don't hate you," she murmurs. We lock eyes, and time slows to a stop like it does sometimes when we're together. We both move towards each other in tiny, subtle movements, like we're a pair of magnets that can't avoid the pull of the other. Her orange blossom and cinnamon scent fills my nose, and my heart squeezes. Her gaze drops to my lips for a second, then snaps back up to my eyes. Is she thinking of kissing me as much as I'm thinking of kissing her?

A knock at the door has us both jumping backward, despite the door still being closed. Annie clears her throat and grabs the handle to open the door. Amber's on the other side to let me know that my next appointment for the day has arrived.

I shake my head to clear the lust from my brain. Annie has already started heading down the hallway ahead of me, following Amber at a quick clip. My eyes follow her as she walks away, taking in the jeans that may as well be a second skin across her shapely thighs and ass.

I swallow hard and adjust myself in my pants before following her to the front desk area where she's putting on her coat. I lean one elbow on the ledge of the tall reception desk and call out to Annie before she takes off out the door.

"See you tomorrow?"

She pauses at the door and looks over her shoulder at me. She takes in my flexed bicep and drops her gaze in a quick perusal. Her cheeks flush as she realizes that I just watched her blatantly check me out. She drops her gaze to her shoes and mumbles that she'll be back in the morning.

I smile to myself once she's gone. The attraction between us clearly isn't one-sided; maybe there are feelings on her side as well. I'm already counting the hours until she's back.

When I decided to make a genuine effort to not be an asshole to Annie anymore, I was hoping for us to be friends. But now? Now it feels like there's a chance for more.

A chance to make her mine.

THE NEXT MORNING, I have Annie's favorite drink sitting on the desk, waiting for her. I may have texted Leena to find out what Annie likes at BIGGBY. Some sort of blue raspberry concoction with red boba at the bottom. She walks into the office and pauses in the doorway. Her eyes instantly find the bright blue drink at her space.

"What's that?" she says, her voice laced with suspicion.

"I think it's something they call a Scuba Blast." I shrug and go back to looking at my laptop.

"I know it's a Scuba Blast. Why is it here?"

"I thought you'd like it. Call it a welcome to the team present."

She narrows her eyes at me and crosses her arms. I can feel her glare from across the small room, but I don't look up.

"Eric," she says in a warning tone.

"I wanted to do something nice." She waits, so I add, "I asked Leena what you liked from BIGGBY. Not a big deal."

I glance up at her and smile. She stares back at me, conflicted and confused. She's studying me like she's trying to figure out if I'm messing with her somehow.

"Am I not allowed to do something nice?" I ask, getting a little annoyed at her suspicion. I've been on my best behavior lately.

She visibly deflates a bit. "I'm sorry, thank you." She sets her bag down and picks up the bright blue drink with a small smile. "I'm still not used to you being nice and, honestly, I'm also not used to work being a pleasant place. I think I'm conditioned to be on edge."

My hackles rise instantly at the hurt tone in her voice. I'm curious as hell about what the fuck happened in Chicago, but I don't think she would appreciate me asking just yet.

"Well, that's not how I run my office. Besides, I had to get that apology gift card for Amber. I'm not usually a dick to people."

She nods, studying me again. "I'm starting to actually believe you on that."

"I'll convince you. You'll see."

She shoots me the first actual smile I've seen from her today and gets to work on the computer. I'm already plotting ways to see that smile more.

Now that we've dropped most of the hostility between us, I want to earn her trust. I have three months of her working here. Wherever she goes next, I want to keep her in my life, and I will do whatever it takes.

"DUDE. WHAT ARE YOU up to?" I slow down the treadmill I'm running on. The Flash let me use their gym facility since I work with the guys. I don't have therapy appointments on Friday afternoons, so I like to start my weekend with a long workout.

I find Bailey and Dan flanking me on the treadmills on either side of me. They're both studying me as I slow down to a jog.

"Just getting my workout in. What are you guys up to?"

"You know that's not what we meant. The girls had drinks last night, so we've heard all about your first week of work with Annie."

I slow my treadmill down even more. "What do you mean? It's been okay. We haven't been fighting."

"No, you haven't. You've been bringing her drinks and having long, tense moments of eye contact."

"I'm trying to be nicer." I try to shrug it off, but they're both staring me down. "There may have been a bit of a tense moment the other day. What... uh... what did Annie say about it?" I try to say it casually, but it doesn't work. I'm too eager to know what they've heard.

They make eye contact with each other around my head, and both break into huge grins. "I fucking knew it," Bailey finally says.

"I don't know what you're talking about."

"The fuck you don't," he says with an eye roll.

"We're talking about your undying crush on Annie," Dan adds with a smirk. "I knew you never really got over her. One week working with her and you're already pining after her again."

I let out a big breath as my shoulders droop. I'm not interested in playing the denial game anymore. Dan and Bailey are coupled up with the two people who are closest to Annie. At this point, it makes more sense to recruit their help than keep them in the dark.

"Ugh. You're right. Do you think it's super obvious?"

I almost laugh as both sets of eyebrows shoot up.

"Whoa. I didn't expect you to admit it," Dan scoffs. "I thought we were gonna have to go through a few more rounds of you denying it before we got here."

"Might as well save us all time and own up to it. I'm into Annie. I always have been." All this open honesty makes my skin prickle with anxiety. I run my hands through my hair to ease it. "I don't want her to hate me anymore. Possibly even like me at some point? It might be too late."

The guys share another of their mind-reading glances. I swear, these two spend way too much time together. Bailey clears his throat.

"I don't think it's too late. But you need to tread carefully. She's been burned, and I think she's still feeling that hurt," he says carefully.

White-hot rage pours through my body at that. The desire to punch the asshole who hurt her floods my veins. I'm not a violent man, but the thought of someone treating her badly makes whatever protective caveman instincts I have flare up. I clench my fists as I continue to walk.

"Do you know what happened?" I grit out, my jaw tight with anger.

Dan shakes his head. "Not our story to tell, Doc. You just gotta go gently. Ease her into being friends before you try getting her into your bed."

"It's not like that, man. I want... more. I don't know." Another pass of my hands through my hair. I'm not going to have any hair left by the time this is all over.

"Hmm, you should probably start as friends. There's a lot of bad blood for you to make up for before she'll trust you," Bailey says gently.

"You're right. Any chance you guys want to help me win her over?" I ask, making eye contact with each of them to show them how serious I am. I'm met with big smiles and pats on the shoulder that almost send me flying off the back of my treadmill.

"Yeah, man. We're in," Dan says.

"You should start by coming out to open mic tonight. Leena said Annie was planning on coming," Bailey adds. His eyes light up suddenly, and he shoots me a devious smile. "Should we discuss what you should sing tonight?"

"You can't be serious?"

Dan and Bailey glance at each other and burst into over-exaggerated evil laughter.

I'm already regretting asking them for help.

THE GUYS WERE, IN fact, not kidding, which is why I'm standing onstage at Songbird's open mic night. Leena smirks at me from the side of the stage as she sets up the karaoke machine to play the song I chose. She nods to give me the go-ahead to introduce myself, so I clear my throat.

"Hi, everyone. Please be gentle. I'm a newbie."

That gets me some chuckles from the crowd as I shift on my feet. The intro music starts, and I take a glance at the bar where Annie sits with Jessie. She watches me with a look that's part curious and part amused. I saw the surprise cross her face when Leena told me it was my turn.

Dan and Bailey said we should be strategic in our song choice and pick something that reminds me of Annie, but also something I already know how to sing to avoid extra embarrassment. So here I am singing "The 1" by Taylor Swift, to a full bar.

I don't want to weird Annie out, so I do my best not to sing it right to her. I do make eye contact with her every so often, though, and her expression has changed. She looks focused and a little confused.

Well, damn. The guys were right when they said she'd figure out pretty quickly that I was singing about her. To her.

As the last notes finish, the crowd cheers for me, and I won't lie, the entire experience has my adrenaline pumping. I go back to my seat, a couple of stools down from her, and order a beer from Cass, the bar's manager. I feel Annie's eyes on me, but I'm trying to play it cool, at least a little bit.

Dan and Jessie hop up to move down to the end of the bar where Leena is setting up the open mic lineup. Shooting a glance down at Annie across the vacant spaces at the bar, I give her a nod and smile, but I don't move stools. I'm doing my best not to come on too strong.

I'm looking down at my phone when I feel her move to the stool next to mine, and I have to bite the inside of my cheek not to smile.

"So, Taylor Swift, huh?" she finally asks to get my attention.

"I'm not ashamed of being a Swiftie." I shrug and shoot her a grin.

"Are you like a full-fledged Swiftie or more of a casual fan?"

"I saw the Eras Tour movie in the theater and caught the Indy tour stop," I explain.

"Really?"

"My sister is obsessed. And honestly, Taylor puts on a hell of a show," I explain.

"Wow. I never would have guessed. I like your sister already," she says, shaking her head and smiling. Dammit. Now I owe Jenna for dragging me into her fandom and helping me get on Annie's good side.

"I contain multitudes, sweetheart."

She rolls her eyes at the endearment but doesn't correct me. I call that progress. Just a few weeks ago, she bit my head off for calling her that.

"Annie! You're up!" Leena calls from down the bar. Annie finishes the drink in front of her and makes her way up to the small stage. My eyes can't help but follow her as she moves across the room. She's wearing tight, skinny jeans and a strappy top that shows off her shoulders despite the icy chill in the air outside.

I take advantage of her being up in front of everyone and let myself take in a full perusal of her curves. Her hair is pulled up into a high ponytail that shows off her slender neck. I can picture having that ponytail wrapped around my hand as I lose myself inside her.

Shit. I need to get my thoughts under control before I embarrass myself.

"Hi there! I thought I'd go with a show tune tonight, so here's 'Maybe This Time' from *Cabaret*."

Leena hits the button for the music, and Annie starts to sing. I know I've heard this song before, but watching Annie and the emotions crossing her face as she belts out the older Broadway number, it feels like I'm hearing it for the first time.

My heart squeezes in my chest with desire. Desire for her, desire to take care of her. My feelings for her are so much more complex than wanting to get into her pants.

The crowd cheers and claps as she finishes the song and hops down from the stage. She comes right back to the stool next to me and plops down. She gives Cass a wave for another drink and then looks up at me with a shy look on her face.

"You were incredible, Annie," I say sincerely.

"Eh, I'm not as good as Leena, but I do like that song." She shrugs and takes a big drink from the glass Cass has brought her.

"No, I mean it. You've got an amazing voice. Don't downplay it."

She gives me a shy smile before plunking her glass down onto the bar and gathering her coat and purse. "Thanks. Well, I'm heading out. See you Monday, Boss Man."

"You good to drive?" I ask as I eye the drink she's just finished in record time.

"Considering that's just Diet Coke, I think I'll be fine." She shoots me a wink and pats my arm. The skin on my arm tingles a bit from where she made contact.

"Wait! I'll walk you out!" I blurt out suddenly, not willing to let her go yet.

Her eyebrows wing upwards, and she tilts her head like she's studying me. "Umm, okay. Let me say bye to Leena and Jessie."

I put my coat on as she gives them quick hugs. She walks toward me, and I notice she's still holding her coat over her arm, so I reach out and grab it to hold it open for her to put on.

She stares at me, surprised for a beat, before mumbling a thank you and letting me help her with the coat. I hold the door open as we walk together into the cold December night.

Chapter Nine

Annie

WHAT THE FUCK? I have no idea what is happening with Eric. I thought he was just being nice at the office because he knows what a clusterfuck his books are and needs me to fix it. But tonight has been a whole other level of nice, flirty Eric. *And that song.* I swear he was singing it to me. Now, he's walking me to my car, and for some reason, I'm letting him. The move with my coat was such a mind fuck.

Why is he acting like a gentleman? What kind of game is he playing?

The silence stretches between us until I clear my throat.

"Big plans this weekend?" I ask awkwardly.

"Nah, I usually spend the weekend staring at my accounting software and pulling my hair out, but now that I have you, my weekend's wide open," he says with a laugh.

"Oh, good! You can come help me move!"

"I can make that work."

"I was kidding. You don't need to help me move."

"No, really, sounds like a good time."

I laugh and shake my head. I'm pretty sure he's kidding about helping, so I let the topic drop.

"You know you didn't really need to walk me to my car. It's only a couple of blocks down the road."

"I wanted to. I don't like the idea of you walking alone at night," he replies.

"This is Fort Starling, and I've spent most of the last five years working past dark and taking the 'L' home," I tease.

"I don't like the idea of you taking the train home alone at night either. But while you're here, at least I can be the one to make sure you're safe."

"Making sure you get those books of yours fixed, huh?" I joke, smiling up at him.

He chuckles, "Definitely that. And I don't want anything bad happening to you. What can I say? You bring out my protective side."

"Oh yeah. You're super protective when you're not the one bullying me." I laugh, but even I can hear the edge in my voice. Eric grabs my elbow and turns me to face him. I instantly feel guilty at the pained expression on his face. "I'm sorry. I shouldn't have called you a bully; neither of us was very nice to the other, and I'll admit I started it at least some of the time."

"Are we ever going to move past college? I'm truly sorry for every time I treated you badly. Do you think you could ever forgive me?"

I blow out a breath of air. "I'm trying. I just... I find it hard to trust people, especially lately. I keep waiting for the other shoe to drop and for you to go back to being an asshole."

"I won't. I promise you that, Annie." He's gazing down at me so sincerely. We've somehow moved closer so that all it would take is a small step forward for us to be touching. We're back in that place where time stands still, and I can barely breathe. He reaches out to tuck a loose piece of hair behind my ear. Is he going to kiss me?

"I'd really like us to move on and be friends," he murmurs, studying my face.

I blink up at him, trying to ignore how much the word "friends" stings right now when it shouldn't. Being friends with Eric is the smart plan. The plan that keeps me from being too invested, too attached. I nod and smile at him as I take a small step back.

"I'd like that. Friends."

We get to my car, and he opens his arms for a hug, so I step into his embrace, pressing my body against his. I wrap my arms around his waist, and he tucks me into his chest and rests his chin on my head. Every instinct in my body wants to melt into him and stay there in his arms, but I force myself to back away. I get in my car and give Eric a small wave as I drive away.

Friends. That's for the best, given our history and our current employment situation. I have a boss boycott to stick to here. But I can't seem to shake the feeling that I want Eric to be more than my boss. More than my friend.

Once upon a time, I wanted him with every fiber of my being, and I don't think that ever truly went away.

I'm so fucked.

The next morning, Mom's doorbell rings just before nine. I open it, expecting Leena, Jessie, and their significant others to help me move into the Songbird, but I'm startled to find Eric on the other side of the door. He's dressed in workout gear, holding a large Krispy Kreme box, and smiling down at me.

"What are you doing here?"

"I told you I was gonna come help you move," he says with a shake of his head.

"I thought you were kidding!"

"No way. Here, I grabbed these. The hot light was on when I passed by, so I had to stop."

He hands me the donut box, and I can feel the heat of the donuts through the cardboard. I eye him suspiciously for a second.

"Did someone tell you?" I ask him, staring him down.

"Tell me what?"

"I may be obsessed with fresh Krispy Kreme. It's a top-tier treat as far as I'm concerned."

"No one had to tell me. That's common sense. I don't keep driving if the hot light is on. It's basically a rule."

"I have never liked you more. Come on in," I say with a laugh.

I lead the way into the kitchen, putting the donuts down and getting plates and napkins out. Handing Eric a plate, I pop open the donut box. I grab a still-hot donut and take a big bite. I close my eyes and let out what can only be described as a moan. It's borderline pornographic.

Eric clears his throat, and I open my eyes to find him watching me. His gaze is focused on my mouth, and I can see the hunger in his eyes, but I'm pretty sure it's not for donuts. That's an interesting development from Mr. Let's Be Friends. I hold eye contact as I finish my donut and lick the glaze off each of my fingertips. Eric's gaze darkens as he watches me.

The atmosphere in my mother's tiny kitchen is palpable as the tension builds between us. I don't know how long we stand there, staring into each other's eyes, the air crackling around us, before he shakes his head and clears his throat again, breaking the spell. I don't miss his subtle attempt to adjust himself in his shorts, and I smirk to myself. Very interesting, indeed.

Wait. What am I thinking? He's my boss, and I'm not going there. I only needed to make that mistake once to learn my lesson. I shake my head to clear the haze of lust and confusion that Eric's presence has created and eat a second donut, quieter.

Shortly after, Leena, Jessie, and their guys show up, and we jump into the activity of moving most of the furniture from my small childhood bedroom into Bailey's truck. The apartment over Songbird is basically just an empty room since Leena moved most of her stuff out. Luckily, she left the small dining table and the couch. I'll have to go back to my apartment in Chicago to get my things if I end up staying here longer than a few months.

The idea of going back to Chicago makes my stomach turn. It's been such a relief not to have to deal with Kevin every day. How am I going to go back to that? Plus, the more time I spend with Leena and Jessie here, the more I realize how lonely I was in Chicago.

No friends, no life outside of the office, and a waking nightmare at work. Why wouldn't I be raring and ready to go back to that? But not going back to Chicago feels like a failure. Like I'm giving up on every bit of progress I've made in the last five years. I don't do failure. If I don't go back, claw my way back up at work, Kevin wins. Can I let him? I really don't know.

Shaking off thoughts of the future, I focus on getting my things set up in my new space. I love my mom, but it'll be good for us not to be on top of each other for the next couple of months. I'll still check in on her a bunch in the next few weeks, especially with Christmas next week, but she doesn't need my help around the clock anymore.

Bailey and Dan have to take off for a team workout, but Leena, Jessie, and Eric hang out to help me unpack. It goes quickly, since I didn't have much to move from my mom's house. Just a few boxes of random things that came with me from Chicago, or I stole from my mom's house.

"Thank you, guys, so much. Let's order some food. My treat," I say finally, when we've unpacked the last box. Leena and Jessie share a quick look that I don't quite understand before they shake their heads no.

"The team is having a Christmas dinner thing tonight that the wives and girlfriends are going to, so we've gotta get going," Jessie says. "Rain check, though!"

Their sudden dinner plans are suspicious, but I say nothing. They give me hugs and say goodbye to both of us before heading out the door and leaving me alone with Eric. I stare at the door Leena and Jessie disappeared through for a beat before turning to Eric.

"So, dinner?" he asks, smiling.

"You don't have to hang out. I'm sure you've got better things to do than get takeout with your employee on a Saturday night," I reply. I'm not entirely sure whether I want him to stay or go. Well, that's not true. I want him to stay, which pretty much means he should go.

"I thought we were friends now?" He smirks down at me with his arms crossed. The stance makes his biceps look huge, and I can't take my eyes off them for a hot second. When I look up into his eyes, his smirk is wider, if that's possible, and his eyebrows are raised. He definitely caught me checking him out. Again. I roll my eyes at him, trying to act casual, but my cheeks are burning.

"Right, yeah, friends or whatever," I mumble as I pretend to arrange kitchen utensils. "So, food?"

"Let's do it. What are you in the mood for?"

"Well, I was thinking I'd order some pizzas for everyone, but since it's just the two of us, we can do whatever." I shrug, racking my brain for food ideas. "Oh! I know! I saw they put in a Penn Station that totally wasn't here the last time I visited. What d'ya think?"

"Love Penn Station. Here, I can order it on the app." He pulls it up on his phone and hands it to me. "Go ahead and put your order in."

I scroll through the menu, trying to decide which sandwich to get. Eric notices my indecision, and I glance up at him.

"I can't decide! I love their Reubens, but the artichoke sandwich sounds so good!"

Eric shrugs, "So get a small of each. No, wait! Get the artichoke in whatever size you want, then we can get a large Reuben and split it. I go back and forth between that and the chicken teriyaki, anyway."

"That sounds perfect." I give him a big smile and input my order, and the shared Reuben. "Here, put yours in, and I'll grab my card to pay for it."

"Don't worry about it. I got it."

"No, Eric, it's my treat since you helped me move," I say, grabbing my purse to get my wallet out. I hold my card out to him, but he ignores me.

"No, Annie, it's my treat because I want to."

"Just let me pay!"

"Too late. I already had my card on the app." He shrugs and gives me that cocky smirk again.

"Fine. I owe you, then. You brought donuts, now you're buying dinner." I put my hands on my hips and glare. He just chuckles at my frustration.

"You don't owe me anything, sweetheart. Come on, let's run into Kroger to grab drinks, and you probably need some groceries for the week, right?"

My stomach drops at both his endearment, which I've stopped fighting, and his thoughtfulness. I'm going to need him to dial back all of this sweet and kind behavior before I melt into a puddle.

"Alright. But I'm buying the drinks. I mean it, Eric." To make my point, I poke my finger at his chest, and it low-key hurts my finger.

Damn, he must be ripped to have such hard pec muscles. *Fuck.* I should not be thinking about how ripped Eric is.

He is my boss; he is off limits. Maybe if I repeat it in my head over and over again, it will stick and I'll stop noticing all the things I like about him now that he's not being an asshole all the time. I shake my head and walk toward the door.

"Let's go, Boss Man."

He chuckles and follows me out the door.

He is my boss; he is off limits. After a few hundred more times, hopefully, I'll believe it.

Chapter Ten

Eric

THIS IS NOT A date, but fuck if it doesn't feel like one. From wandering the grocery store together, taking our sandwiches back to her new apartment, to now sitting together on her small love seat watching reruns of *The Office* on the tiny TV we moved from her mom's house, every part of tonight has been perfect. It's shockingly comfortable to spend time together, now that we're not fighting constantly.

The ease and connection that flowed so perfectly between us the night we met are back now that we're not at war. It makes me want to kick myself for being such a dick for so long. Maybe if I stopped being an ass back then, she would have realized I was the better option for her over that douchebag Scott. Instead of punishing her for choosing him, I should have fought for her.

I shake my head to clear the regrets so I can focus on now. Now, she is sitting less than a foot away from me on this tiny loveseat, enjoying a companionable silence while we watch one of the greatest shows ever made.

I turn myself a bit and put my arm up along the back of the seat. Not touching her, but invading her space. After just a couple of heartbeats, she shifts in her seat to lean ever so slightly into me. The guys warned me to go slow, and given our history, I refuse to rush whatever this is that's happening between us.

Another episode passes, and I take a risk and scoot close enough that we're right up against each other. I hold my breath and wait for her to move away, but she doesn't; she settles in a little closer. I drop my arm down around her shoulders, and she leans her head back onto my chest.

I could get used to this. I can picture us spending our evenings just like this. Yes, I want to get her into bed and do some extremely not-safe-for-work things with her, especially after that stunt she pulled earlier with the donut, but this right here is what I really want. I'm ready for more than casual hookups and meaningless flings.

Eventually, I feel her nodding off. I'm not going to press my luck and try to stay the night, so I gently nudge her awake.

"Sweetheart, I'm gonna take off so you can get to bed," I murmur in her ear.

Annie jumps to her feet, "Oh my god. I'm so sorry. I can't believe I fell asleep on you!"

"It's no big deal. It's late." I pocket my phone and wallet and head toward the door, with her following behind me to the door. She crosses her arms over her chest and yawns. She looks exhausted, and I feel a little bad for staying so late, but I didn't want to leave. "I'll see you Monday?"

"Yep, I'll be there," she says as she smiles up at me. I open my arms for a hug, and she steps into me, wrapping her arms around my waist. I hold her for a long moment, wishing I didn't have to go. Wishing she were mine.

She leans her head back to look up at me, but doesn't let go of my waist. "Thank you again. For everything. I'm really glad you were here today." The heat builds between us as she gazes up at me.

"I'm glad I was here, too." Is this it? Is this my moment to kiss her and show her how much I want to be with her? I lean my head down, getting ready to move in for a kiss, but she jumps back.

Ouch. Not going to lie; that stings. She looks a bit embarrassed, and she's not making eye contact. *Fuck.* I hope I didn't make her uncomfortable. I swallow down my hurt feelings and plaster a smile on my face.

"Go to bed, sweetheart. I'll see you Monday." I turn to the door and have my hand on the knob when I hear her in almost a whisper.

"I'm not your sweetheart."

Fucking hell. Two steps forward and one huge step back. I pretend I didn't hear her and walk out the door. I don't want her to see how disappointed I am with the way the night ended.

As I get behind the wheel of my car, I lean my head against the seat and let out a big, shaky breath. That goodbye sucked, and I don't understand why. The night was going so well; I was sure we were headed in the right direction.

I drive home and replay the night in my mind. If anything, it confirmed two things. The first is that the guys were right. I need to take things super slowly with how skittish Annie is. And the second is that more than anything, I want Annie to be mine.

I'm not giving up. I'll take it slow, but until she tells me she's not interested, I will do everything I can to win her over.

Sᴜɴᴅᴀʏ ɴɪɢʜᴛ, ᴏʀ I guess Monday morning, my phone wakes me out of a dead sleep. What the fuck is happening?

One look at my phone screen tells me that someone has deactivated the alarm at the office. I get an alert anytime it's armed or disarmed. I look over at my alarm clock for the time. Who the fuck is at the office at four in the morning?

I drag myself out of bed and pull on my work clothes. Whatever is happening at the office, I figure my day is starting, so I might as well just get ready. What a great way to start a Monday. I pull up to the office to see Annie's car parked out front, and I'm even more confused. Why would she be here in the middle of the night?

When I open the back door of the building, I can hear music coming from the office. Ever since that first open mic where Annie played the guitar, I've been listening to Saving Jane on repeat, so I instantly recognize the song. Annie is singing along loudly, and she clearly didn't hear me open the back door.

I walk silently to the office and peek into the doorway. She's got her back to me and is facing the computer, working in the accounting software she had me download last week. I watch her for a few seconds, working away and singing along to "Happy" before I clear my throat loudly.

She jumps in her seat and screams as she spins around. She's clutching her chest and glares at me hard when she sees me leaning in the doorway, smirking at her.

"Jesus Christ, Eric. You scared me," she scolds. "What the hell?"

"What the hell are you doing here at four in the morning?" I ask grumpily, still not happy about being woken up so early. I'm also still salty about the way she jumped back when I leaned in for a kiss the other night, and it's not helping my mood.

"How did you even know I was here?"

"I have it set up so I get alerts on my phone when the alarm is deactivated. It woke me up."

"Well, what does it look like I'm doing? I'm working. I couldn't sleep..."

Her shoulders slump in defeat, and I suddenly realize her eyes are puffy and red, like she's been crying. All annoyance drains away and is immediately replaced with concern.

"What's wrong? Are you okay?"

"I'm fine," she says, but she sniffles, and her eyes fill with tears.

"Annie, you're obviously not fine. Talk to me, sweetheart." Her face crumples at that, and she starts crying in earnest.

"It's so fucking stupid. I don't even know why I'm crying." She wipes at her eyes. "How much did the guys tell you about my boss in Chicago?"

Alarm bells go off in my head as she continues to sniffle and wipe her eyes. I hand her a tissue from the box on the desk and take my usual seat across the desk from her.

"Not much; they were pretty tight-lipped about it," I say carefully. "Something about him being an asshole."

"Accurate," she grumbles. "He called me last night. Ugh, this is so embarrassing. So, almost a year ago now, I had a bit of a fling with my boss. It didn't end well, and he immediately moved on with my co-worker."

I clench my fists tight under the cover of the table, trying to keep my face neutral as she tells me about this jackass. I already want to punch him, and I'm pretty sure this story is going to get worse before it gets better.

"I lost my temper in front of everyone, and he's basically been punishing me ever since." She gives me a sad shrug as she uses the tissue to wipe her eyes.

"Punishing you how?" I grit out with my jaw clenched tight. I'm furious this dickhead dared to treat her so badly.

"He forced me into this three-month leave instead of the three weeks I had planned on, for one. And he's been slowly giving my clients to Serena, his girlfriend." She lets out a bitter laugh. "Actually, I guess she's his fiancée now. That's why he called me yesterday."

My entire body is clenched with tension. Is she still hung up on this jerk? So much that she's been reduced to tears at him being engaged? Is that why she jumped away from me the other night?

"So you're upset that he's engaged? Are you... do you still..."

She figures out what I was trying to ask and starts shaking her head adamantly. "No. I do not still have feelings for that twat-waffle and I don't care that he's trapped Serena, queen of the office bitches, into a lifelong, probably orgasm-less existence. I'm upset because he's trying to push me into quitting."

"What do you mean?"

"He said now that he and Serena are engaged, it would probably be pretty awkward to have me there in the office. He said it would be best if we made my leave of absence permanent."

"He's firing you because he got engaged? How does that make sense?"

"That's just it. He can't really fire me. He wants me to quit. I'm so frustrated that he's trying to manipulate me and is winning because I'm not sure I want to go back, but I don't want Kevin to get his way either."

I'm livid at this poor excuse for a man for treating Annie this way, but I'm also relieved she doesn't have feelings for the bastard.

"I'm sorry this is happening to you. None of what he's doing to you is okay."

Annie blinks at me for a moment and sniffles again. "Thank you for saying that. It's such a shitty situation. I kept tossing and turning all night, so I finally gave up on sleep and came here to get some work done. Working with the numbers helps."

"Well, I'm glad my nightmare of a bookkeeping mess can be of assistance."

"Math makes sense. It makes me feel smart and capable, instead of insecure and inadequate."

"He's the inadequate one if he let you get away," I say with a vehemence that startles even me. Annie studies my face for a minute before a sad expression crosses her face. "What?"

"Nothing. I've just yet to meet a man who wanted to keep me. Kevin is the latest in a long line of men who are interested at first, only to decide I'm not worth the trouble. My dad. Even you."

I'm stunned by her confession, but also confused. I'm about to ask for an explanation when she gets up and grabs her purse.

"Anyway, I don't want to talk about it anymore. It's almost six now, so I'm going to swing through the BIGGBY for some caffeine. Do you want your usual?"

I clear my throat and nod. "Yeah, that would be good. Thanks."

She nods and scurries out the door. I stare after her. What does she mean, I decided she wasn't worth the trouble? I searched the campus for her for months. She was the one who dated my roommate without giving me a chance. Yeah, I was an asshole to her after that, but she was the one who rejected me.

Soon, when she's less upset, I'm going to ask her what the hell she meant. I have to get to the bottom of this. Because if she thinks for one second that she's not worth the trouble, I will do anything and everything in my power to prove her wrong.

Chapter Eleven

Annie

AFTER MY EMBARRASSING, TEAR-SOAKED confessions last week, and a small break for Christmas, things have been lighter between Eric and me. There's an ease between us that wasn't there before. A trust was created by my confiding in him and his comforting me rather than judging.

I actually love working through the puzzle that his previous office manager made of the books. She has original records linked in the wrong places, and as far as I can tell, not everything was billed that should have been. Some patients were even overbilled. It's a mess, but it's been fun to untangle everything.

I'm digging through a pile of mail that was opened but clearly not sorted with any kind of rhyme or reason when I find a letter from the IRS. I read it three times as dread fills my body.

Fuck. The IRS is saying that the practice hasn't filed taxes correctly for the last several years. We have to submit records and receipts to prove the filings are correct, which they probably aren't. It says Eric's practice owes the IRS an eye-wateringly huge amount of money in back taxes. The deadline to turn everything in is next week, at the end of the year.

"Eric!" I call out loudly. He's out on the floor, but last I checked, he didn't have any patients out there. He must hear the panic in my voice because he pops right into the office.

"Annie, you okay?" He looks so concerned that my heart squeezes in my chest.

"I'm fine, but the practice may not be. Did you see this letter when it came in?"

He takes the paper from me, and the blood drains away from his face, and he collapses into his chair. With his elbows on the desk, he runs both hands through his hair. He looks like a distant relative of Albert Einstein when he finally looks up at me. His eyes are shiny, like he's on the verge of tears.

"Annie. What do we do? I... worked so hard to start this practice... I can't..." His voice breaks, and I reach across the desk to grab his hand.

"We will figure this out. I promise, Eric. We can fix it. I will call the IRS hotline now to see what they're looking for, and we will get the filings fixed. I can do this. We can do this."

He swallows hard and squeezes my hand. "Thank you."

I squeeze his hand back and take a big breath, steeling myself for the sheer amount of work that has to happen in the next week. I meant what I said. I will fix this for him. My drive to protect and take care of Eric is startling, but I try not to think about what that means. I don't have time to analyze my feelings right now. I have to get to work, saving his business.

THE NEXT WEEK FLIES by in a flurry of paperwork and extremely long nights. I spend almost every waking hour not spent checking in on my mom, working on the practice's books. My contact at the IRS gave me a detailed list of documents to prepare and ways to correct the previous years' filings.

Eric has been right by my side the whole time. We make an amazing team. He may not be able to help with every aspect of the bookkeeping, but he's been here sorting documents by date, printing records, and helping organize all the pieces. Any moment he's not with a therapy patient, he's in the office helping me make sense of everything.

We even called Fred in to help with some of the more daunting accounting work. He could give us a few hours during the week before he went on his trip. I definitely owe him a lunch to thank him for all of his help.

Finally, the last pieces we need are all put together and packaged in a hefty envelope. I take it to the post office myself on Wednesday afternoon and have them weigh it and schedule it for overnight delivery to make extra sure that we meet the Friday deadline.

I pop back into the office, tracking information in hand, to let Eric know I dropped everything off. Amber lets me know as I'm passing the front desk that the therapy appointments are done for the day, and she's heading out. She and Tasha were stars this week too, handling everything they could to free up Eric's time. We'll have to bring in breakfast for them sometime soon.

We. I pause as I realize just how much I've been thinking of Eric and me as a unit. After this week, we feel like a team. It would be so easy to slip right into thinking of us as partners. I need to remind myself that he's my boss. This is his business, and in a couple of months I'll be either headed back to Chicago or looking for something new.

I wander back to the office to look for Eric since I don't see him out on the floor. I find him in his desk chair, hunched over with his arms crossed on the desktop, his head resting on his arms.

He's fast asleep. I can't blame him; we've been working nonstop to get everything ready to send to the IRS, and neither of us has slept much this week. I could practically see the stress of trying to save his practice sitting on his shoulders like a weight this week.

I stop in the doorway and study him for a moment. He looks younger, softer around the edges, asleep like this. He's always handsome, but when he's asleep, there's something vulnerable about him. It reminds me of the eighteen-year-old version of him I used to know, but without the cocky asshole veneer. The urge to take care of him presses on me, and my heart squeezes.

He must sense me watching him because he startles awake. He smiles when he finds me in the doorway. I can feel my cheeks heat at being caught watching him sleep.

"Paperwork is on its way," I say to cover my embarrassment.

"Great, thank you so much for everything this week. I know an IRS emergency wasn't part of our original deal." He rubs the sleep out of his eyes.

I wave him off. "Our deal was that I would fix your bookkeeping. The taxes were part of that. When tax season rolls around next year, we'll be ready for them."

I pause and realize I just implied I'd still be working here a few months from now. God, I kind of like that plan. I could always pick up other bookkeeping and accounting clients. Maybe do freelance or set up my own firm.

Of course, that means Eric may be my boss for a long time, which means I need to nip this attraction I have for him in the bud. He can be my boss and my friend, but more than that is off the table. No matter how much I want it.

"Still, let's grab some dinner to celebrate being done with that paperwork." He stands and walks toward me with a big smile, and I can't say no.

We end up picking up Chinese food from my favorite place and take it back to his place. His house is small but cute, with a wrap-around porch that would be perfect for a comfy chair in the summer.

The inside is tidy and warm, not at all what I would expect for a thirty-year-old man who lives alone. The front door opens into his living room with a cozy-looking couch and recliner aimed at a large TV. Throw pillows and blankets are draped along the couch, giving it a homey feel.

"Your house is so cozy," I call out as I spread out all the food containers on his coffee table. I open them while he grabs plates and utensils from his kitchen.

"That would be my sister Jenna's doing. She insisted that if she was going to come hang out here, she was gonna be comfy. I told her she didn't need to hang out here, and she laughed at me and kept decorating like it was her house."

"She sounds awesome. It must be nice having a sibling. I always wanted one growing up, but Leena and Jessie filled that void when we finally met in middle school."

"I forgot you guys have been friends for that long. Now that I think of it, you do all act like sisters. Definitely explains Jessie's matchmaking obsession with Leena and Bailey."

I bark out a laugh at that. "Yeah, Jessie went a little crazy with that one."

He chuckles and shakes his head. "What should we watch? *The Office* again, or do you want to mix it up?" he asks, turning on his TV. "I just restarted *Brooklyn 99,* if you want to watch that."

"Let's go with *Brooklyn 99.* I'm about due for a rewatch."

He smiles at me as he starts the show and settles in on the couch beside me.

Fuck. I shouldn't be here. It's too tempting to settle in and enjoy Eric's company. He is still my boss. He could be my boss for a long time if I don't go back to Chicago.

Off limits, off limits, off limits.

But I don't move. My brain screams at me to get out of here, but my heart and body are full-on ignoring it. I eat my fried rice and focus on Andy Samberg's antics as Detective Jake Peralta rather than on the man next to me.

When I'm done eating, I tell myself to get up and leave. But I don't. I settle deeper into Eric's couch, scooting closer to him instead of away. It's like the night he moved me into my apartment. We're drawn together, slowly closing the space between us.

I knew he wanted to kiss me that night, could see it in the way he leaned in. I almost let it happen, but I jumped back at the last second. The hurt that crossed his expression after I moved back killed me, but I need to stick to my guns here. I need to stick to my boss boycott for my own well-being.

I turn to tell him I'm leaving and find him already looking down at me. Our faces are inches apart. For all my inner monologuing, there's no resisting him this time. He searches my eyes and dips his head, and I lean into him. Our lips meet gently at first, but we both instantly move to deepen the kiss.

He turns his head and slants his mouth over mine to swallow the gasp that escapes me when he pulls me into his arms. Through all the hostility between us, this is what I've wanted from the moment I met him over twelve years ago. I've pictured this moment more than I would ever admit out loud, and now here it is.

His hand moves into my hair as he deepens the kiss, running his tongue over the seam of my lips. I open to him, brushing my tongue along his. My hands are fisted in the front of his shirt. This kiss is just as good as I imagined. Although I never imagined he'd be my boss when we finally gave in to the tension between us.

He's my boss. What if things end badly and we go back to hating each other? What if this implodes my career... again? I'm just starting to envision a new future for myself here in Fort Starling. What if this tanks my reputation and I can't get accounting clients? I pull back and stand up, but Eric follows, holding onto my hands.

"Annie..."

"We can't... I can't do this." Looking up into his eyes, I can see the sadness and confusion there. "I'm sorry. I can't keep getting involved with whoever I'm working with. That bit me in the ass before, and I can't do it again."

"I am nothing like your asshole boss. You know I'd never treat you like that."

"I know. But this could still end badly. We were so hostile for so long. I don't want to go back to that. If I don't go back to Chicago, working at your practice is all I have. I can't keep putting myself in this position."

"But you can walk away from this? This connection. I have never felt this way about anyone. I felt it the night we met, and whatever spark was between us then is still there. Don't tell me you don't feel it, too."

"Of course I do. I always have. But it didn't stop you from walking away the first time, and I can't take the risk. It's too much. I'm sorry." I grab my purse and flee out the front door. Thank God, I followed him to his house in my car, so I don't have to wait for an Uber.

As soon as the door shuts behind me in my apartment, I let myself break down. I cry for the hurt I caused Eric by shutting him down. For the missed opportunity of seeing what we could be. And I cry for my eighteen-year-old, starry-eyed self who thought she met her soulmate.

She might have been right, but the thirty-year-old version of me is too chicken shit to find out. I cry myself to sleep, mourning what could have been.

I DO NOT WANT to go out tonight, but I don't have a choice. Bailey called me early this morning to fill me in on his plans to propose to Leena tonight at open mic. Jessie and I are supposed to convince her to go out for a girls' night, only to drag her to the Songbird.

The convincing part was super easy; she was all for our plan to get ready at her house, then go out. I offered to drive, so she didn't have to, and she was thrilled. Now it's the putting on a happy face and going through the motions of getting ready that is low-key killing me.

Tonight is about Leena and Bailey, so I refuse to share all the bullshit that is happening in my personal life right now. My heart hurts for the way I left Eric the other night. The vision of his sparkling blue eyes, full of pain, has haunted me over the last couple of days. But I slap on a smile and act like I'm excited for girls' night.

Leena is super confused as we walk up to Songbird. "Why are we here? I thought we were going out for girls' night?" she asks as we approach the door. "I wouldn't have gotten dressed up if I knew we were going to the bar I own!"

I roll my eyes at her, and Jessie shakes her head as we each hold on to one of her arms, dragging her through the doors of the Songbird Cafe. We're taking our job of getting her here seriously.

"Cass said there's an open mic act she thinks you'll like. We can still go out after," Jessie lies.

"Oh, alright." Leena shrugs. "At least we drink free here!"

Cass appears to get Leena a drink. She's in on the entire plan, so she gives Leena shit about drinking free to stall and keep Leena's focus. When Leena asks where the open mic act is, Cass pretends to look around, knowing full well Bailey is the act and is hiding in the kitchen.

"I think they went to the bathroom," she says and shrugs. "I'll get it going in a few minutes."

Leena nods and glances around the room, looking happy and content. I'm so happy for her, but I can't help but feel a pang of jealousy. All the pieces of her life are coming together while all of mine are falling apart.

As Cass steps onto the stage to announce the start of open mic and give Bailey his intro, I feel my phone buzzing. I accidentally elbow Leena, trying to get it out of my pocket. My heart stops for a beat as I see Eric's name lighting up the screen. I swallow hard but realize Leena is watching me, so I roll my eyes and decline the call.

"What was that?" she asks, with my eyebrows raised.

"Just Eric. It's like he doesn't realize it's a Friday night and his employees are out having lives," I lie with fake exasperation, knowing Eric was probably calling to talk about what happened the other night. I haven't been in the office for the last couple of days. I told him I needed a break to rest a bit after the IRS craziness, but really, I'm not ready to face him after I ran from his house.

She nudges me and waggles her eyebrows at me suggestively. "Maybe he wasn't calling as your boss? Maybe it was a booty call."

I haven't told her what's been going on with Eric and me, but she's always claimed there was chemistry between us, despite the hostility. She doesn't know just how right she is, but I have to deflect or I'll start crying. It's her night. I'll fill her in another day.

"I told you that is not happening. I learned my lesson in Chicago. I'm never sleeping with my boss again," I insist. No matter how much I want to be with him.

"I mean, is he technically even your boss? You're helping him out more as a favor than as an actual employee, right?" Leena presses. She's not entirely wrong, but she's not right either.

"He's paying me to clean up the mess he and his old office manager made of the books. That makes him my boss. Bosses are off-limits." I chug my drink and hope that will be the end of the discussion.

I can see her out of the corner of my eye, studying me, and I know she wants to say more, but luckily, I'm saved as Bailey's voice comes through the microphone.

"Hi, everyone! My name is Bailey Turner, and I want to dedicate this song to the love of my life, my sunshine."

Leena spins on her stool and gasps. Her jaw drops as she takes in Bailey standing on the stage with the microphone in his hand. An instrumental version of John Legend's "All of Me" plays over the speaker, and Bailey starts to sing.

He's pretty good, and Leena looks absolutely stunned. I'm guessing she didn't know he could sing. I hope he likes being up there because he'll never be able to get out of performing with her now.

When he finishes the song, he puts the microphone back on the stand but waves Leena up to the stage. She walks up in a daze, shaking her head. She pokes him in the chest, and we can just barely hear her voice coming through the microphone next to them.

"Where has this been for the last year and a half? You know you're going to have to do duets with me now, right?" she says emphatically.

"I'll sing duets with you for the rest of my life if you say yes." With that, he sinks to one knee and produces a small velvet box from his pocket.

Leena gasps as we all cheer. At least now I'm crying happy tears for my best friend.

I can see Bailey talking from his spot on his knee as Leena nods and wipes her eyes.

"Yes! Of course yes! I love you so much!" she replies loudly enough that it echoes through the mic. We all cheer and clap for the happy couple.

The guys from the Flash materialize from the kitchen area where they were hiding, and my heart stops as I make eye contact with Eric. I should have known he would be here, but I didn't even think of it.

Shit, that's probably why he was calling me.

I drop my eyes quickly and focus back on Leena. Tonight is about her, and I will do my level best to ignore Eric while she's still here. I can feel his gaze on me, but I don't look up.

Tonight is about Leena and Bailey. Later, when everyone is gone, I can go back to breaking down.

Chapter Twelve

Eric

I'M HAPPY FOR BAILEY and Leena, and I'm glad Bailey invited me to be here for his proposal, but I can't focus on anything but Annie tonight.

With her hair curled around her shoulders and some kind of dark makeup lining her eyes, she looks radiant. She's wearing a sparkly top under a leather jacket with the skinny jeans that cling to the curves of her ass perfectly.

She also looks sad, which I'm guessing has to do with me, but I'm not going to approach her until the happy couple has left the building.

I can't get what she said Wednesday night out of my head. She said I walked away from her, and I can't figure out what she means. I'm done waiting for her to explain herself. I need to know what she meant and set the record straight.

She's the one who keeps rejecting me. She rejected me back in college when she started dating my roommate without even talking to me. Annie knew just where to find me, knew Scott was my roommate, and she chose him. She's the one pushing me away now.

Every shitty thing I did back in the day was a direct reaction to her moving on without giving me a chance. I know that doesn't excuse my assholery, she didn't owe me anything. But it still doesn't give her the right to say it was all on me.

Leena and Bailey hang around for a couple of hours before they disappear out the door hand in hand. I look back at Annie and watch her visibly deflate, her shoulders sinking and her smile dropping. Looks like I'm not the only one who was trying to stay upbeat for appearances.

She leans over and says something to Jessie. They hug briefly, and I see Annie disappear behind the bar and into the back kitchen area, where the stairs to her apartment are. I drain my drink and move to follow her. We're getting this settled tonight.

I jog up the stairs and take a deep breath before I knock on her door, hard. I can hear her moving around on the other side of the door. She has a peephole in the door, so I'm sure she's trying to decide if she's going to ignore me or let me in.

"Come on, Annie. I want to talk," I say a little more gruffly than I should, but at this point, I'm too frustrated to keep my tone in check. I hear her flip the lock, and the door opens.

"What do you want, Eric?" She glares at me and raises her chin in defiance. Apparently, she's choosing hostility, too. Looks like we're falling back on old habits.

I roll my eyes and edge past her into her apartment. She clenches her jaw as she steps back to let me pass, and I see her roll her shoulders back as if she's prepping for a fight. She slams the door shut and crosses her arms, waiting for me to start. I don't want to fight with her, but I'll be damned if I don't get an explanation.

"I want to know why you keep acting like I was the one to reject you in college. You were the one who wasn't interested in me after that night, but you said I walked away. I need to know what the fuck you meant," I grit out, doing my best to not raise my voice.

"That's bullshit!" Her eyes spark with anger. "You had my number. You never called."

"I did not have your number! You left before I could get it!" I'm pissed now. She's rewriting history and painting me as the bad guy. "I looked for you for months. I went back to fraternity parties and constantly looked around the oval and the union for you. I didn't find you until you showed up in my room with my fucking roommate."

"That's not fucking true! I left my number with... oh god." The blood drains out of her face, and her eyes well with tears. "Fuck. Scott never gave you my number, did he?" Her voice is little more than a whisper as she studies my face.

"No, he didn't even tell me he was in a class with you, even though he knew I was looking for you."

"No. That first night. When Leena needed to leave, I wrote you a note with my number and gave it to Scott to give to you. He said he would. When you didn't call or text, I was devastated. I thought we had such a strong connection. I thought for sure you felt it, too." Tears slip down her face as she wraps her arms around herself. "After a couple of months, Scott and I were paired up on a project, and I got up the courage to ask him if he knew why you never reached out. He said you weren't interested, that you had a girl staying with you."

I'm stunned for a moment. I knew Scott was an asshole but I didn't realize just how deep his betrayal went. I tug a hand through my hair as I put the pieces together.

"He was lying. I was hung up on you for weeks. Scott knew all about my search for you. I talked about you all the time, and I never brought girls back to the room." I clench my fists tightly at my sides. If I ever see Scott again, I'll throttle him.

"I saw you, though," she says through her tears, sniffling and wiping at her eyes. "Scott told me you'd be with her at a party. I saw you with a tiny blonde. You had your arm around her. I bailed as soon as I saw you. A few weeks later, Scott asked me out, and I said yes, mostly out of spite."

"That doesn't make any sense!" I run my hand through my hair again, as I rack my brain, trying to figure out who she saw me with.

It hits me all at once. Jenna visited my freshman year during one of her breaks. She stayed with me in the dorm so she could feel "nostalgic" since she had moved into an apartment for her junior year. Her tiny liberal-arts school didn't have Greek life, so she begged to go to a fraternity party that weekend.

I search my phone for a picture of her and hold it up for Annie to see. "Was this her?"

She squints at the phone and nods. "Yeah, I think so. Who is she?"

"Jenna, my sister. She was visiting for the weekend and wanted to go to a fraternity party. *Fucking Scott.* He knew she was my sister. He lied to you to make me look bad."

"Oh, my god. He manipulated everything to get what he wanted." She covers her eyes. "*Fuck!* I only dated him to piss you off. I never understood why my dating Scott made you mad when you weren't interested in me."

"I was pissed off at you for choosing him. He knew how I felt, and he gloated often. I spent that entire year miserable anytime I had to be in my room. If you weren't there, he brought you up."

"Fucking Scott."

"Fucking Scott."

We stand still, silently staring at each other as the weight of everything we've just discovered settles over us. My asshole ex-roommate lied to and manipulated us and we blamed each other. Years of anger and hostility, and neither of us knew why the other was pissed.

After a moment, the mood shifts between us. We're still standing a couple of feet apart, staring, but the tension between us thickens. We reach for each other at the same time, our lips crashing together.

This isn't the slow, careful kiss of the other night. This kiss is us both unleashing the months and years of anger, hostility, and lust. It's raw and hungry, both of us clutching at each other. Making up for lost time. It's a kiss full of untapped rage and pent-up frustration.

I walk her backward and push her against the door. I press my hips into hers, showing her how much I want her right now. She loops her arms around my neck, pressing her chest into mine. I reach down and lift her legs, hauling her against me. She responds by pushing up into my arms further, wrapping both legs around my waist.

Her pants turn to moans in my mouth as I turn and carry her over to the bed. Her apartment is one open room, with a small bathroom off to the side, so it's a quick trip from the door to the large bed in the corner. I lay her down and stretch my body over hers, careful not to rest all of my weight on her.

Her hands make their way down the front of my shirt as she unbuttons it. I roll off to the side and cover her hand. Her eyes flutter open, confused by my pause, but I have to be sure she really wants to do this. I search her eyes as I tuck her hair behind her ear.

"Annie. Are you sure you want to do this? You were so against it a couple of days ago."

She studies me for a long moment. "Everything is different now. I'm sure. I want you, I've always wanted you."

She pulls me back down to her, holding my face in her hands as she kisses me long and slow. I move my hand under her top and up her smooth belly. My fingers are met with bare skin where I expected to find a bra. I groan into her mouth as I find her nipple and roll it between my fingers, making her moan and writhe.

I travel kisses down her neck while pushing her top up. She sits up a bit to pull it over her head. I'm met with a view of her small round tits, her nipples a delicate pink. I'm overcome with the need to taste her, so I pull her nipple into my mouth and give it a gentle bite.

"Please. Eric. I need more." Annie moans and squirms under the attention I'm paying to her breasts. She tugs at my shirt, trying to pull it off. "Get this off. Too many clothes."

I chuckle, amused that she's been reduced to incomplete sentences before I roll off her and stand up. I finish unbuttoning my shirt and pull it off. She slides forward on the bed and reaches for my belt. I let her unbuckle the belt and pop the button on my jeans before I grab her hands.

"Be patient, sweetheart," I smirk down at her, and she shoots me a defiant look that only makes my erection push even harder against my jeans.

"I've been waiting twelve years for this. I can't be patient." Her eyes shine with desire, and I push her back onto the bed, leaving my jeans on but unbuttoned. I'm hanging onto my control by a thread, and if I lose my pants now, I know I'll snap. I need to make this good for her first.

"I've been waiting twelve years for this, too, and I want to make it last."

I reach for her jeans and pop the button. She lifts her hips and helps me to slide the tight jeans down her legs, taking the silky thong she wears with them. I run my hand down her soft belly to the small landing strip of light brown hair between her legs.

She gasps and opens her legs for me as I find her wet center. I swipe around her clit, not quite giving her the pressure she needs based on the frustrated noise she makes.

"You're so wet for me, sweetheart," I say as I slide a finger inside of her. I can feel the walls of her pussy already clenching and spasming around my finger. I add a second finger and use the first finger of my other hand to press on her clit. It doesn't take long before she's writhing and moaning under my hands.

"Oh fuck, Eric. I'm gonna...oh god." She thrashes her head as her pussy clamps down on my fingers. I almost come in my pants, imagining being buried inside her tight, wet heat. I pull away to get rid of my jeans and pull my boxer briefs down, but then freeze as I realize I don't have a condom with me. My cock bounces free as I stand still in my indecision.

Shit. I'm not one for random hookups, so I never keep them with me. I run a hand over my face.

"What's wrong?" Annie asks as she notices my pause and sits up. "Do you not..."

"I don't have a condom," I grit out. "I'm sorry, I just realized it."

I bend down to pull my pants back up when she stops me with a hand on my hip. She wraps her hand around my hard length. She gives me an experimental tug, and I drop my head back with a groan. When I look down at her, she meets my gaze as I move my hand to cup her jaw. She places her hand over mine, and I bend to capture her lips again.

"I have an IUD, and I haven't been with anyone since I was last tested. So I'm all clear if you want to..." she murmurs against my lips.

I gulp at the thought of taking Annie bare. I pull back to make sure I can look into her eyes. "I'm all clear, too. Are you sure?"

She nods and pulls on my hand, bringing me back down to the bed.

"I'm sure. It's better this way. I don't want anything between us."

Fuck. I swallow hard and kiss her. Her hands roam through my hair for a moment until she moves one down to grasp my cock again. She gives me another tug, this one a little harder than before, and I moan into her mouth. She runs the head of my cock against her clit and through her folds, gathering moisture, before lining me up at her entrance.

I push my hips forward slowly, focusing hard on not losing control as I'm surrounded by her tight heat. I see her grimace in pain, and I go still.

"You okay?" I ask as I move her hair out of her face.

"Yeah, it's been a while. You're bigger than I'm used to." She gives me a mischievous smile, and I smirk down at her. She moves her hips, encouraging me to move. "Okay, keep going. I'm good."

I take it slowly, entering her inch by inch until I'm fully seated inside of her. We're both breathing hard as I pull back and push all the way back in, making us both moan together. I pick up the pace as she meets me thrust for thrust. I can feel the walls of her pussy starting to spasm again, squeezing me.

"Oh my god, I'm gonna come again," she moans out, sounding surprised. I pick up the pace a bit, wanting to come with her. I'm right at the edge, and I can feel my balls tighten, a tingle starting at the base of my spine. Reaching one hand down between us, I use two fingers to press on her clit and she explodes around me.

Her pussy clamps down on me hard and breaks through the last of my control as I pour my orgasm into her. I keep pumping slowly until we're both spent. I bend down and kiss her slowly before gently pulling out of her.

"Don't move, sweetheart." I run to the bathroom and find a wash-cloth, which I run under the warm tap. I come back out to the bed to find her with an arm thrown over her eyes, still breathing hard. "You alright, Annie?"

She lets out a disbelieving laugh. "You've only ruined me for anyone else and blown my mind. Sure, alright sums it up."

I chuckle as I gently clean us both up with the warm washcloth. After tossing it back on the sink in her bathroom and killing the kitchen light that was on this whole time, I climb into bed next to her and pull her comforter over us.

I reach for her and gather her into my arms. She rests her head on my chest as her hand rests on my stomach. I kiss the top of her head and let out a contented sigh.

"Don't worry. You've ruined me for anyone else, too."

I drift off to sleep with her soft laughter playing in my ears and the woman of my dreams in my arms. Finally.

Chapter Thirteen

Annie

I WAKE TO FIND myself still wrapped up in Eric's muscular arms. The wave of happiness at finding him still in my bed is laced with fear.

Are we together now? Or was this just us scratching a decade-old itch? If we're not going to be together, could I possibly keep working for him? I'm realizing this is the exact reason for the boss boycott. I really don't want to look for a new job while I'm still wavering about going back to Chicago in a couple of months.

"Take a breath, sweetheart. You're spiraling, aren't you?" Eric grumbles sleepily.

"No way. I'm totally chill and not freaking out at all."

He chuckles right into my ear, sending chills down my spine. God, I want to keep this man. I don't want this to be a fling. I want it to be the real thing.

"What are you thinking about?"

"Oh you know, just obsessing about everything from tonight, wondering where we go from here, worrying about how to handle my job in Chicago and, of course, fantasizing about throat punching both Kevin and Scott for being manipulative pieces of shit."

He's quiet for a beat. Probably trying to figure out the best way to escape my apartment.

Shit.

"Let's tackle those in order. What are you obsessing about? Do you... Do you regret what we did?" There is hesitation in his voice as his body tenses around me.

"No. Not even a little."

"Good. Me neither." He relaxes a bit, and I realize he was nervous about that answer. He's still tense; maybe he's still nervous. "Where do you want to go from here?"

Now it's my turn to be nervous. I can sense the tension running through his arms as he waits for me to answer. But what if his answer is different from mine? I take a deep breath and tell the truth.

"I want us to be together. In a full, actual relationship. Not a fling or a hookup," I say quietly. "I'm ready for more, and I'd like that to be with you. If that's what you want, of course."

All the tension vanishes from his body as he lets out a huge breath. "Oh, thank God. You had me worried there. That's exactly what I want."

"Really?"

"Yeah, really. I did the casual hookup thing for a while, but now that I'm older, I'm ready to move on from that. I tried the dating apps for a bit, but I didn't hit it off with anyone. My sister thinks it's because I was comparing everyone to you. It'll kill me to admit to Jenna, but she was right."

It's dark in the room, but you could probably see my smile from space. Despite all the other bullshit swimming through my brain, at least this piece of happiness is mine to claim.

"Well, I guess a lot of the rest of it doesn't matter then. That was the most important piece of the puzzle." I relax back into his chest, a little more at peace than I was before. "And for the record, I think I was doing the same thing. I wanted to be in an actual relationship so badly that I'd tell myself it didn't matter that the spark was missing. But I knew what that spark felt like thanks to you, and no one ever lived up to it. Especially not Kevin."

"Can I ask what actually happened with him? You gave me the broad strokes before, but if I had the entire story, I could help you figure out what to do from here."

I sigh. He's right. I'd rather he knows everything, even if it's embarrassing to tell. I go through all the details of my fling with Kevin, from thinking it was going to be more, to his manipulations, and trying to get me to quit.

"I don't want to go back to work there. It just also feels like I've failed, and I hate that Kevin gets away with everything."

He's quiet for a long moment. "What if you quit but also file a complaint of sexual harassment as your reason for resignation? So, yeah, he technically gets his way, but there will also be a formal complaint against him."

"I guess I could. His mom is the managing partner of the firm, so I don't think it will do much good. I don't know. I'll consider it. My leave is set up through early March, so I have a good two months to work through it."

"We'll figure it out. I'm in this with you."

"Thank you." I snuggle back into his chest, feeling drowsy and happy.

"You're welcome, sweetheart. Get some sleep."

He kisses the top of my head, and I drift back to sleep, thinking this may be the happiest I've ever been.

IT TURNS OUT THAT when you're finally in a relationship with the only man you've had an instant connection with, life is very, *very* good. And life being good makes me super suspicious.

It's a lesson I've learned several times over. If something seems too good to be true, it probably is. I'm always waiting for that second shoe to drop. This is probably why now that I'm at lunch with the girls, I'm downplaying what's happening between Eric and me.

"So, you guys are like 'together' together? He's your boyfriend?" Jessie asks with her eyes narrowed.

I shrug, like Eric and I haven't spent every waking moment, and most of the non-waking moments, together for the last two weeks. "Yeah, I would probably call him my boyfriend."

"Well, Dan seemed to think Eric was pretty serious about you." My head snaps up to look at her, giving me away. Jessie spots my reaction instantly. "Ha! I knew you were full of shit, playing it all cool! It's serious, isn't it?"

I shrug again, this time in a wave of insecurity.

"Why are you downplaying it, Annie?" Leena murmurs.

"Ugh. I don't know." I bury my face in my hands.

"Okay, start again. The truth this time," Jessie says, crossing her arms.

"I like him. I've always liked him, I guess."

They both roll their eyes at me. "We've only been saying that for twelve fucking years," Leena scoffs.

"I know!" Burying my face, I groan into my hands. "I just got my feelings hurt, and so did he. We took it out on each other, and because we were stupid kids, we never talked it through. Fucking Scott. If I ever see him again, I owe him a kick to the balls."

Leena and Jessie both laugh at that. They hadn't been Scott's biggest fans back in the day.

"That fucking tool," Leena growls out. "I always hated him. He was sleazy. I hated the way he looked at you. Like you were his possession. So smug."

"I know. The smugness makes so much more sense now that I know he manipulated me and tortured Eric." The very thought makes my nose scrunch in disgust. I hate how easy I was to manipulate. And Kevin is a clear indicator that I haven't learned all that much since college.

Why do I have such terrible taste in men? What if Eric is a mistake, too?

"Stop that," Jessie says suddenly, pointing at my face.

"What?"

"I can see you spiraling. I can see you doubting this thing with Eric. Babes, I know shitty men have hurt you in the past, but Eric won't be one of them. Not now that everything is on the table."

"Like, I know that intellectually, but I'm having a hard time believing it. I'm waiting for everything to blow up in my face."

"That's fair and a completely understandable reaction," Leena says, squeezing my hand. "Just don't let it get in the way of letting Eric in. I really think he's one of the good ones. Try to have a little faith."

I nod, taking in her words. Leena learned a similar lesson not that long ago, so she's probably a reliable source to take advice from.

"Okay." Jessie claps her hands and slaps a huge binder on the table in front of Leena. "Should we talk wedding planning?"

Leena rolls her eyes, but excitement hides in them. I'm sure she wants to rein in Jessie's enthusiasm. It won't work, though. Jessie owns an event planning company, and she looks downright giddy at the thought of one of us finally getting married.

I smirk at Leena, and she shoots me a mock glare. She'll pretend not to be into Jessie's planning mania, but we know better. I'm so happy for her, but also a little jealous. It's like that scene in *Friends* where Rachel and Phoebe are talking about being happy for Monica getting married. I'm mostly happy for her and a tiny bit jealous.

Hopefully, someday it will be my turn, but I can't think about that right now. Can't afford to get my hopes up, because if I do, it will hurt that much more if everything comes tumbling down.

"How was lunch with the girls?" Eric asks as I walk back into the office. He stands up and helps me pull my coat off, only to turn me into his arms for a lingering kiss.

"It was good. Jessie strong-armed Leena into doing some early wedding planning."

"I'm not at all surprised by that."

I pull back so I can head to my seat at the desk, but Eric holds onto my hips, keeping me pressed against him. He lowers his head and runs a soft kiss along the side of my neck. I close my eyes and tilt my head to give him better access.

I quirk an eyebrow at him. "Should we really be doing this here, Boss Man?"

His eyes darken as he pushes me backward to move closer to the office door. He flips the lock as he presses me into the door. His hands move into my hair as he peppers kisses along my jaw.

"Our appointments are done for the day, Tasha cleared out, and I told Amber she could take an early day too. It's just us here, and I've been picturing bending you over this desk all week."

Eric's teeth nip my ear, sending chills down my spine, as my breathing and heart rate pick up the pace. I would be lying if I said I hadn't pictured us doing it here. This week, and before we got together. My hands travel up his chest to the nape of his neck, where I thread them into his hair to pull his face down to mine.

"In that case, show me where you want me."

He lets out a low growl as he grabs the lapels of the blazer I'm wearing and peels it off me before turning me around to reach the zipper of my dress. I press my hands into the door to give myself some leverage so I can push my ass back into him.

Eric drags my zipper down slowly, tracing the path down my spine with his fingertips. He pops the closure on my bra, and I let both the dress and bra pool to the ground, leaving me in my cheeky lace underwear and the knee-high boots I love for cold winter days.

"Let's lose these," Eric murmurs in my ear. He slides the panties down my legs. "The boots stay on."

"Whatever you say, Boss Man."

"Good girl, now go sit on the desk and spread those legs for me."

I didn't have Eric being a dominant alpha type in the bedroom on my bingo card before we got together, but I'm not mad at it. The people pleaser in me is very into his bossy vibes, while the defiant streak I have makes it extra fun to push his buttons and challenge him.

I cross the room to the desk, adding some extra sway to my naked hips. I take a seat at the edge of the desk but instead of spreading; I cross my legs, lean back on my hands to push my boobs out and raise an eyebrow at him. He studies me, his eyes blazing.

Eric stalks toward me slowly, his eyes tracking up and down my body. He places his hands on the desk on either side of my hips as he leans his body into mine.

"I thought I told you to spread these legs," he growls into my ear.

"Maybe I wanted you to do it for me." I shoot him a mischievous smirk and wait.

"Hmm. I guess I can do that for you, sweetheart." He trails his fingertips down my body on their way to my legs. He gently presses on my knees to open my legs, lowering himself to his knees between them.

"Oh god," I whimper as his hot breath caresses my core. He swipes his finger through my folds and I cry out as his tongue connects with my clit. My hips buck involuntarily, trying to get closer to his mouth. He lets out a low chuckle at my eagerness that vibrates through my pussy, intensifying the wave of lust rolling over me.

Eric presses one hand into my abdomen, holding me down on the desk, as he slides two fingers deep inside and uses his tongue to make hard flicks against that sensitive bundle of nerves. Lightning races through my veins as my entire body clenches. He builds me higher and higher, thrusting his fingers inside me as my inner walls spasm and clench down. He finally pulls my clit into his mouth and gives it a hard suck, shattering my world.

I unravel completely, vaguely aware my hands are clenched in his hair for leverage as I ride his face until I'm completely sated and boneless. Finally, as I come back down to earth, he gives my clit one last kiss before he pulls back and stands up. He cups my face and kisses me long and hard. I can taste myself on him, and it only turns me on more.

Wordlessly, I reach for his belt buckle and undo the zipper on his slacks. I push his pants down along with his briefs, freeing his perfect dick. I give him a hard tug before Eric surprises me with a quick turn, so I face the desk.

He gives my shoulder blades a soft push and I fold over the desk, bent over for him, ass in the air. Wearing nothing but my knee high boots and a smile. It's so hot. This is easily the most turned on I've ever been in my life.

"Fuck, Annie. You're so perfect," Eric says as he runs his hand down my spine. He runs the head of his dick against my clit, ramping up the throbbing in my center. I let out a whimpering moan as he lines himself up at my entrance. With one powerful thrust, he pushes all the way inside and pauses. I try to grind back against him, but he holds me still with his hips.

"Please. Eric, I need you to move," I gasp out, continuing to grind back against him, seeking friction. He groans softly as he pumps in and out of me. The angle is deeper than any we've tried over the last week, and he's hitting just the right spot that I'm already close again. "Oh god, I'm so close."

"I'm right there. Come with me, Annie."

The second orgasm takes over, and I literally see stars behind my eyelids. I always thought that was an exaggeration for dramatic people and romance novels, but I'm experiencing it now in real life.

Eric pulls out of me and collapses into the desk chair. He pulls me down to sit sideways on his lap so he can wrap his arms around me. We hold each other for several long minutes, catching our breath in a companionable silence. Finally, he kisses me on the temple and murmurs in my ear.

"Let's go home. We can order in and watch a movie."

I turn my head to look at him and catch his eyes widening as he realizes that he just referred to his house as my "home," and he looks like he's waiting for me to freak out.

The thing is, I'm not freaking out. His house somehow already feels like home to me. I decide to let his comment slide, not wanting to dig into why I feel at home there or how it will feel if this all blows up in my face.

I don't want to think about how much I'll lose if this goes sideways, because that list keeps growing. With every day, I fall a little bit more in love. Not just with Eric, although I'm definitely falling hard for him, but with the life we could have together.

I shoot him a smile and get myself cleaned up and put back together. As we walk out into the frosty night together, I remind myself to stay in the present. To not get ahead of myself with visions of the future. To keep my hopes down.

To remember that this could all come crashing down.

Chapter Fourteen

Eric

MY SISTER'S CAR IS the first thing I spot when we pull into my driveway. Annie rode home with me, so she glances up at me, concerned when I swear under my breath.

"What's going on?" she asks. "Who's here?"

I sigh. "My sister, I'd like to apologize in advance for anything crazy she says to you. I love her dearly, but she's nuts."

Annie grins at me and leans in to kiss me on the cheek. "I'll be the judge of that."

She pops her door open and bounces out of the car. After all the stories about Jenna I've told her over the last few weeks, Annie is brimming with excitement to meet her. I let out another enormous sigh, knowing I'm in for a night of merciless teasing. There's no way these two don't gang up on me.

They're already chatting and hugging when I get out of the car. My sister turns and gives me a mischievous grin.

"Look who decided to get out of the car after all. We were wondering if you were going to hide out there all night."

"Hi, Jen Jen," I say, letting out a big sigh. Jenna's eyes light up, and I realize I've already made a mistake by using her nickname. *Shit.*

"Hi, Icky."

Annie makes a choking sound at that. "Wait, Icky?" she asks, already holding back laughter.

Jenna cackles as I open the door to the house. I go immediately to the fridge to grab a beer. It's going to be a long night with these two.

"When I was little, I couldn't say 'Eric'. The only thing that came out was the 'ick', which of course became 'Icky'. Our moms thought it was so funny that it stuck. They don't use it much anymore, thanks to *someone's* whining, but I can't resist."

Annie laughs hard at that. I can already see the wheels turning in her head enough to be sure she's going to call me that damn nickname. Probably in public.

Annie runs to the bedroom to change out of her work clothes. She's left a few things here over the last few weeks, so I'm cornering Jenna while I can.

"What are you doing here, Jenna?"

She smirks up at me from her perch on the couch. "I have wanted to meet Annie for years. You've been officially dating for weeks now. Did you really think I would wait around?"

No, but I hoped. I wanted to stay in our bubble for a little bit longer. I roll my eyes at her. "You staying for dinner?"

Jenna grins, knowing she's won. I doubt Annie would even let me kick her out at this point. I heard them murmuring about baby pictures as we were coming up the walkway.

"Of course I am, baby brother. I've got a future-sister-in-law to bond with," she says sweetly. "I've got so many stories to share with her!"

I chug the rest of my first beer and crack the top on a second one, leaning against the kitchen counter. I pinch the bridge of my nose and start scrolling through the delivery apps to find dinner. If I'm going to endure this torture, I'm going to need food.

Annie walks into the kitchen and laughs. "Why do you look like you're about to face a firing squad?"

She wraps her arms around my waist and rests her head against my chest, giving my collarbone a sweet kiss. The tension of knowing my sister is about to embarrass me eases a bit, wrapped in Annie's arms. I kiss the top of her hair and loop my arms over her shoulders.

"She's here to embarrass me and you know it." I sigh.

"She's here because she loves you and wants to get to know the person you're spending all your free time with. If you think about it, this is your fault."

"How do you figure that?" I quirk an eyebrow at her, waiting for an explanation.

She smirks. "How many times have you ignored her FaceTimes in the last few weeks?"

I groan. "I hate it when you're right. It was only a matter of time."

"You love it when I'm right." She pushes up on her tiptoes to kiss me before stealing my beer and sauntering out of the kitchen.

I laugh and shake my head, grabbing another beer for myself and one for Jenna. I consider hiding in the kitchen, but Jenna's voice calling from the living room kills that plan.

"Icky! Come on out here! The embarrassing stories aren't as much fun if I can't watch you squirm."

They both laugh, and I take a deep breath before joining two of the most important women in my life for an evening of torture. I wouldn't want to be anywhere else.

MULTIPLE PIZZAS AND A tray of cinnamon sticks have been devoured when there's finally a lull in the embarrassing storytelling. Annie and Jenna are both curled in the corners of the couch, and I was relegated to the recliner.

"Oh, Icky, before I forget, Mom wanted me to ask if you're going to Steve's birthday party this year. He invited them, and Mama Vee wants to go, but only if you're good with it."

I sigh and shrug. My moms have always taken my side in the sperm donor drama, but they've been his friend for a long time. And regardless of his not being fit to be a father, he throws incredible parties.

"I'll call them. We're on mostly good terms these days. I thought they knew that."

"They do, but they're still making sure you're okay with everything."

"Who's Steve?" Annie asks sleepily.

I pause before answering, and Jenna's eyebrows raise. "Our dad," I say simply.

Jenna scoffs. "Our sperm donor," she corrects. "I've never thought of him as our dad."

"I know, Jen Jen."

"On that note, I'm heading out." She gets her boots on and starts bundling into her coat and hat. She gives me a tight hug and whispers in my ear. "I understand why you love her."

I squeeze her back. Partially as a show of affection, but more as a warning to keep her voice down.

She chuckles as she walks away from me and pulls Annie into a tight hug of her own. She whispers in Annie's ear, too, and the two of them dissolve into giggles again.

I roll my eyes at them, but deep down, I love that they're getting along so well. My sister is my best friend. It would be a problem if she didn't get along with whoever I marry.

Shit. That thought is best kept to myself. Jenna is rubbing off on me with all of her premature future-in-law talk.

Jenna heads out, and I lock up for the night. Annie is dead on her feet as she gets ready for bed. I can see the exhaustion pulling on her as she pulls one of my shirts over her head and climbs into bed.

When we're snuggled up in the dark of my bedroom, Annie curls into my body with her head on my chest. She asks the question that has obviously been on her mind since our earlier conversation with Jenna.

"Can I ask what happened with your dad?"

I let out a long breath. I figured she'd want more information after Jenna brought him up. "Steve was my moms' friend from college. When they decided they wanted to have kids, they wanted a sperm donor they knew rather than going to a bank. Steve was charismatic, smart, and fun, but not interested in the idea of raising kids, so he felt like a perfect choice for them. They used his sperm to have Jenna, then again with me two years later."

I pause because this is the part where things get a little more complicated for me. Annie must sense my hesitance because she starts to trace circles on my chest in a soothing pattern. I pat her hand and continue.

"My moms are amazing. They love us so much, and I'm lucky they were the ones to raise me. But as a teenager, I started really wondering about my dad. The guys I was friends with had these awesome dads who took them fishing and coached their sports teams, and in my head, I built Steve into this perfect dad.

"When I was eighteen, my moms agreed to introduce me to him. Steve traveled around for work and had finally moved back to Columbus, so they reached out to him. He told them he didn't want to meet me."

Annie sucks in a breath, her body tensing. "Oh, Eric, I'm so sorry."

I run my hand through her hair and kiss her forehead. "Thanks, sweetheart. I was, of course, heartbroken by the rejection. And in hindsight, I would guess that it factored into how upset I got when I thought you chose my roommate over me. I think rejection was a major trigger for me at the time."

"Oh, my god, that makes so much sense. You were already hurting, and then you were told that I wasn't interested. No wonder you were an ass."

I chuckle at that. "I know. I'm sorry."

"It's okay. We're past all that now." She leaves a soft kiss on my chest. "You said you're on good terms with Steve now. How did that happen?"

"He contacted me a few years later. He said he felt bad for blowing me off, but my guess is that he just wanted to tell his alumni buddies he had a son at The Ohio State. Steve has always been focused on what other people can do for him.

"It took a long time and several years in therapy for me to accept it. He's not going to transform into the perfect dad I always wanted. This is who he is, and it's up to me to decide if I want him in my life or not."

"And do you?"

"At this point, I don't seek him out. I'll answer if he calls me, but I don't put energy into an actual relationship because I know it will be one-sided."

She nods at that. "I've considered looking for my dad. To ask him how he could just walk away. I get leaving Mom, but I can't quite wrap my brain around how he could leave his kid behind. I probably should spend some time in therapy myself." She huffs out a humorless laugh.

"Do you think you will? Look for him, I mean?"

"No, probably not. He bailed and didn't look back. He doesn't deserve any of my time or energy. I may do the therapy thing, though."

"I highly recommend it."

We're quiet for a moment, both contemplating our respective daddy issues. Just when I think she may have drifted off, she murmurs.

"I'm glad we can talk about things like this."

"Me too, sweetheart. Me too."

I WALK INTO THE Flash training facility to find Bailey and Dan both hard at work. The guys are gearing up for spring training next month, so I'm here to work with them and a few others on the team. Making sure they're season-ready.

"Hey Doc! You're looking happy these days!" Bailey calls out with a shit-eating grin on his face.

I grin back at him, unable to hide my contentment. Annie and I haven't spent a night apart in almost a month. She's completely turned things around at the office on both the financial side and the organizational side. She gets along great with Amber and Tasha. Even with the dark cloud of the IRS decision looming over us, I'm feeling good.

Dan and Bailey follow me to the training room to get started on their PT. I study Dan for a minute. His brow is furrowed as he stares at the floor, like he's trying to work out a problem in his head.

"Everything good, Dan?" I ask finally. His head snaps up to look at me like he didn't even realize he was lost in thought.

"Yeah, why?"

"You were staring a hole in the floor. I'm surprised to see you here, actually. Didn't you say a couple of weeks ago that you're retiring?"

"Uh, yeah, that's the plan. Just want to keep this shoulder loose."

I nod, but he's definitely acting weird. I can't help but press him a bit. "How's Jessie doing? She ready to have you in her space year-round?"

Dan cringes. "Yeah. She's been pushing me to retire for years now. We're gonna start trying for a baby. She better be fine with me being in her space," he grits out in a slightly bitter tone.

I glance up to meet Bailey's eyes. He winces, too, and shrugs. Everything's off about Dan today, but there's not much we can do if he doesn't want to talk about it.

"What about you? Are you ready to retire?" I ask gently as I test his shoulder movement.

He looks me in the eye for a long moment before answering quietly, "No. But I don't really have a choice."

I decide not to press the issue any further with him. I get him going on a new exercise for his shoulder and move on to Bailey's knee.

"How about you, star pitcher? You ready for the season?"

"I'm doing good. It's gonna be tough being away from Leena, though. We really got used to being together all the time during the off-season. It's gonna be like an entire piece of me is missing when I'm on the road."

"Isn't that how it's supposed to be?" I grin at him. I see Dan stiffen in his seat, but he doesn't say anything.

"Is that how it is with you and Annie?" Bailey quips back, eyebrows raised.

"Yeah. That's exactly how it is with Annie and I am fucking glad I'm only traveling with you guys for occasional games."

"You've got it bad, Doc." Bailey pats me on the shoulder, and I smile at him before setting off to find the rookie, who I guess isn't really a rookie anymore since he's going into his second season in the majors.

I replay Bailey's words as I work through the afternoon's appointments. He said I've got it bad. Really, I've got it good. And I mean to keep it that way.

Chapter Fifteen

Annie

I'm working through a spreadsheet of patients and their respective billing dates when Eric gets back from the Flash PT appointments.

"Hey, sweetheart," he murmurs as he leans down to kiss the top of my head. "How's it going?"

I smile up at him. It's going so well that I can't stop the panic rising under my ribs. Everything seems so perfect right now. Sure, I haven't figured out what to do about Kevin and my job in Chicago. But things with Eric are excellent. It can't possibly last, right?

"It's good. Just figuring out who's been billed and who still needs to be invoiced."

"Are we able to see when all of their appointments were? I hate the idea of these patients getting surprise bills way after they've been done with PT for months or longer."

"I was thinking about that. I think we should add a letter with the invoices explaining why they may see a bill now. Maybe give them the option of extended payment plans or even waiving the charges depending on the amounts and how long it's been."

"I think that's a good idea. I don't want to be a burden to people just because we had clerical errors."

The temptation to tell Eric I love him is so powerful right now. It's still a little startling to see how wrong I was about him for so long. I always thought he was an asshole, but he's actually one of the most genuinely kind men I've ever met. The way he treats his staff and his patients, really anyone he meets, makes me love him more and more every day.

I do love him, but I'm too afraid of the whole concept to share that with him. Once I say it, I can't take it back. It'll be out there. While I'm pretty sure he feels the same way, there are a million other things that can go wrong. I don't want to put my whole heart on the line here only to have it demolished.

"Any word from the IRS yet?" he asks, brow still furrowed as he scrolls through the spreadsheet I was working on.

"No, not yet. They move pretty slow over there."

I swallow hard, thinking about what could happen if their decision doesn't come back in our favor. I don't think Eric could continue to run the practice if he ends up owing a huge amount. I promised him I would fix it. How could our relationship possibly work if I couldn't?

Eric glances down at his watch. "Oh, hey, it's after five. Why don't we get out of here?"

"Sure. What do you think of hitting open mic tonight? I haven't been since Leena and Bailey got engaged a few weeks ago."

"Let's do it. We can grab some food and head over there. I just want to stop and change before we go." He heads toward the door to grab our jackets.

I could use some Leena time. She's always been the one to tell it exactly as it is. Maybe hanging out with another happy couple will help me get some of this anxiety to loosen its chokehold.

I gaze up at Eric's brilliant white smile and dazzling blue eyes. I want to keep him, but I'm not sure how to convince my brain he'll actually stay. I guess I'll have to enjoy him while I have him. The thought gives me an idea.

"You know, before we go... We have this empty office all to ourselves..." I trail off while dropping my hand to the buttons on the front of the blouse I'm wearing.

His gaze sharpens on the movement and stalks closer to me, jackets forgotten. "Oh really, what did you have in mind?"

"I have some ideas. Here, why don't you sit down? I can show you."

He takes a seat in the office chair, and I use the armrests to lean my body over him. His eyes are at the perfect height to be staring straight down my shirt. I make quick work of the rest of the buttons. Mentally high-fiving myself for wearing my front clasp bra this morning, I pop that open too, and he makes a low sound in the back of his throat as he reaches for me. I dance back out of reach. I have a plan for him.

"Ah ah. Keep those hands on the armrests, mister, or I'll tie them there."

He raises his eyebrows at me taking charge like this, he doesn't object, and his eyes blaze. His hands grip the armrests of the chair.

"Out of curiosity, what do you think you'd use to tie them?" His voice comes out in a low growl.

"Hmm... I guess I'd have to get creative." I raise one eyebrow as I slide my panties down my legs without removing my skirt. I set them delicately on the desk, a warning that I'll tie his hands to the chair if he gets grabby. His eyes darken even more, the crystal blue turning a dark cobalt.

"Now, where was I? Oh yes." I drop to my knees between his legs and reach for his belt. "This belt would make a good restraint too... In case you're getting ideas up there." I glance up at him to find a pained expression on his face. He wants to grab my hair so badly, to take control. Not yet.

I slide down his zipper and pull his pants down just enough to free his erection. He's already hard and ready to go, the tip of his dick leaking just a bit with precum. I lean my head forward to taste him.

"Annie, you don't have to— Christ!"

I lick a swirling path around the head of his dick, making him clutch the armrests of the chair and involuntarily buck his hips.

I meet his eyes. "I want to."

He lets out a shaky breath and gives me a sharp nod, and I get back to work. Pun intended. I swirl my tongue around his head another time before flattening my tongue and sliding the length of him into my mouth. His pants turn to moans as I give him some experimental sucks before lowering down and taking him to the back of my throat. I gag and my eyes water, but I focus on swallowing, pulling back a bit, and then doing it all again over and over until Eric is writhing in the chair, his voice gone hoarse.

"Annie... please. Let me touch you."

I nod, and he threads his hands immediately through my hair. Gripping tight and guiding my mouth where he wants it.

"Oh fuck... Annie...I'm gonna come..."

He tries to pull back, to pull out of my mouth but I hold his hips steady and clamp my lips around his length, giving him a hard suck. I meet his eyes, and his salty release instantly hits the back of my throat. My eyes water all over again as I focus on swallowing it down.

When he finally collapses back in the chair, spent, I slowly pull away, licking up his release. His hand is still in my hair, running gently through the strands. He gazes down at me with such adoration in his eyes that it makes my heart stutter for a moment.

"Fuck, sweetheart. I have no words. I'm pretty sure you scrambled my brain."

"That was the plan."

"Come here." He pulls me off the floor and into his arms. "You are the most incredible woman I've ever met. And I'm not saying that because you just sucked my soul out through my dick."

We both laugh hard at that. I'm hit with another wave of realizing how amazing our connection is. We can go from serious, hot and heavy, to laughing in the space of seconds. The fear of losing all of this licks up my spine again, and I shiver.

Eric mistakes the shiver for a chill and moves to put my clothes to rights. "Come on, let's get changed for open mic, and then we can get food. Don't think for a second I won't be returning the favor on that little 'you can't use your hands' game."

"Oh, really?" I smirk at him as I button my blouse and pull my coat on.

"Really. I have plans for you later tonight."

I chuckle under my breath. I can't wait to see what he has in mind. But first, Songbird is waiting.

WE'RE SITTING AT THE bar picking at what's left of our Taco Bell spread when Eric gets a FaceTime from Jenna. I snatch his phone from his hand and answer it.

"Hey girl!" I chirp into the screen. Jenna's face lights up with a grin.

"Ah! Annie! So much better than my grumpy brother asking why I'm calling," she singsongs into the phone.

"I can hear you!" Eric gripes from beside me, and Jenna rolls her eyes.

"Love you, Icky! What are you guys up to?"

"We're at the Songbird Cafe, waiting for open mic night to get started," I say with a smile. "What about you?"

"Oh. My. God. I've always wanted to go to that! I was gonna ask if you guys want to hang out tonight..."

"Yes! Come meet us here!" I squeal into the phone. Eric cringes, knowing he's in for a night of teasing if his sister joins us.

"Imma get ready real quick, then I will be there, bestie." She hangs up without another word.

I turn in my seat to grin at Eric. He pretends to be annoyed, but I know he's enjoying the fact that I get along well with his sister. Grabbing his phone back, he texts her to let him know when she gets here so he can escort her from the car. He doesn't want her walking from her car in the dark.

I get another pang of Eric feeling too good to be true. He's so sweet and protective. Something has to go wrong. There has to be some mysterious bad habit I haven't encountered yet.

Not fifteen minutes later, Jenna texts, and Eric pops out the door to go get her. As he disappears from view, Bailey plops onto the stool on my other side.

"Hey Annie, how's it going?"

I smile at my best friend's future husband. "It's good. Really good. Almost too good?"

His eyebrows wing up. "What do you mean?"

"I keep waiting for something to go wrong. Like I'm in that part of the book right before shit hits the fan, you know?"

"So what you're saying is you're not letting yourself enjoy how well things are going because you're too busy panicking about potential issues in the future?" He quirks an eyebrow at me and smirks.

I huff out a laugh. "Well, yeah, when you say it like that, it sounds ridiculous."

"Eric is a genuinely good guy. I think it's safe for you to be all in here, A."

I smile at his use of my nickname. Bailey and I haven't known each other long, but I love him for Leena. "I know that. It's just hard to quiet the voices in my brain screaming at me to protect my heart."

"I get that. The problem there is, if you spend too much time trying to protect your heart, if you avoid opening it completely to love, you'll end up breaking it yourself. And you'll break his heart too."

As he says that, Eric comes in the door with Jenna. He shoots me a blinding smile, like he is so excited to see me, even though he was only gone for a few minutes.

Bailey leans down to murmur one more piece of advice. "Keep your heart open Annie, he'll take care of it."

I smile up at him as he stands from the stool and goes across the room where Leena is chatting with a group of bar patrons. I came here for Leena to tell it to me straight, but Bailey's words of wisdom hit the spot. Jessie did a good thing for all of us when she set them up.

I stand up to hug Jenna. "I'm so glad you're here! I can't believe you haven't been to a Songbird open mic yet!"

"I know, I kept meaning to, but I'd always think of it when it was too late to get myself together and out of the house or the wrong night. You guys got lucky, I left the house earlier today, so I was already wearing real clothes."

"So lucky," Eric deadpans from his seat at the bar.

Jenna snickers at him. "He's already grumpy, and we haven't even started teasing him yet."

"He knows it's inevitable. Do you want to perform, or just watch? Either way's cool, especially for your first time." I smile at her. "You could always bust out some Taylor Swift like your brother did."

Eric closes his eyes, cringing and preparing himself for his sister's reaction to that. I can't help but chuckle to myself at their antics. I love how much they love each other.

"WHAT? What song did he sing?"

"He went with 'The 1' a few weeks ago."

Jenna studies Eric for a moment, and even though he's keeping his eyes forward, trained on the bar, I can tell he can feel her staring. A pink blush spreads up his neck from the collar of his shirt.

"Well... I can't imagine at all what message he was trying to send with that one."

Eric's shoulders twitch a touch closer to his ears, and we both dissolve into giggles at his discomfort. I slide between his stool and my own to lean my head on his shoulder and wrap my arms around his waist. Some of the tension eases out of him at my touch. I push up onto my tiptoes and drop a smacking kiss onto his cheek.

"Don't be mad, Icky," I say in a syrupy sweet voice. Jenna cackles behind me at my use of his nickname. Eric closes his eyes and tilts his head back as if he's praying for strength. When he opens his eyes, he finds Cass across the bar.

"I'm gonna need a shot of whiskey. Please."

Cass smirks at the desperation in his voice but pours his drink quickly.

"Come on, Jenna, let's leave Icky to his drink and go ask Leena if she has any ideas of a song we can sing together."

I start to step away from Eric, but he grabs my arm and pulls me back into him for a long, lingering kiss, the taste of whiskey strong on his tongue as he licks it between my lips to press against my own. I step away from him in a daze and link my arm with Jenna's as we walk across the bar to where Leena is perched.

"Damn girl, that would have been hot if he weren't my brother."

I bark out a laugh at that. "It was definitely hot. I have a feeling I'm gonna be in trouble later, and I gotta tell you I am looking forward to it."

Jenna laughs again. "It's so nice to see him so happy. I'm excited to get a sister out of the deal. Oh! Let's see if she has 'Sisters' from *White Christmas*!"

I laugh at her joke, but her words hit me like a bullet. Sister. Does she think Eric and I will get married? We haven't once discussed marriage; it's too soon for that. There's way too much that can happen between here and something as serious as vows and legal ties. Even if we did get married, that doesn't guarantee we'll stay happy together. Just look at my parents.

The panic from earlier is back in full force. I do my best to swallow it down and enjoy open mic, but it looms in the back of my mind like a ticking clock, counting down to heartbreak.

"MOM?" I CALL OUT as I come in the side door. It's been a month since her surgery, and she's been doing great. I mostly stop by just to catch up now, rather than checking up on her.

"Hey, baby girl, how ya doing?" she asks as she comes into the kitchen. She still uses her cane when she's out in public, but she doesn't need it around the house. I can tell she feels so much better now that her knees aren't a constant source of pain. She'll only get stronger as both new knees continue to heal.

"I'm good. How's the knee?"

"Oh, the incision's still a little tender, but it's feeling much better. You let Eric know I'm still doing all of my exercises."

"I will, Mama." I grin at her casual mention of Eric, and her gaze sharpens.

"How is Eric these days?" I haven't told her we're dating yet, but I think she has her suspicions.

"He's good." Once again, I can't keep the cheerful smile off my face.

"So, you're together now?" She moves to the stove to put the kettle on for tea. We've always done our gossiping about my relationships over a cup of hot peppermint tea.

"How do you do that?"

"For one, you're practically glowing, baby girl. I'm not sure I've ever seen you this lit up. For two, I stopped at the Songbird for coffee the other day and Leena spilled the beans, or what do the kids call it? The tea?"

I laugh at that. "Dang, Mom. I was about to give you credit for reading my mind."

"I can still do that. Don't doubt me."

"Never," I say with a laugh.

Once the tea is made, we both take seats at the cozy kitchen table.

"So, tell me how it's going. You look happy."

I sigh. "I am. Extremely happy. So happy I'm terrified it can't possibly last."

"Hmm. You always were a worrier."

"Were you... nevermind." I shake my head. We don't talk about my dad often, so I'm not sure I really want to bring him up now.

"Was I what?"

"Were you and my dad this happy? At one point?"

She lets out a big breath and looks out the kitchen window while she thinks about my question.

"No. I don't think we ever were." My eyebrows shoot up, but I don't say anything. I wait for her to explain. "Your dad and I... we were never really a good fit. We started dating because our parents wanted us to. We were both so fixated on our careers and school, it was easier to stay together than to find new partners, so we stuck with it.

"When you were born, it got harder for us to balance what we wanted for ourselves and what you needed. We lost both of his parents in the space of a year, mine had passed before you were born. We didn't have a lot of help and two big jobs. I was willing to make changes. To do what was best for our family, for you. He wasn't. Finally, he decided he'd be happier moving on. I thought about fighting for him to stay in your life. In the end, I decided it was better for you to have no dad than one who didn't want to be there. I still worry I made the wrong choice."

She studies me as if she's looking for the wounds left behind from their choices.

I clear my throat and blink at the tears that are filling my eyes. "I think you made the right choice, but that didn't stop me from being damaged by his. It didn't stop me from wondering why I wasn't worth staying for."

"I know, baby." She squeezes my hand. "I hate that you've had to deal with that. But you should know his leaving had nothing to do with your worth and everything to do with his inability to think of anyone but himself."

"I know that, intellectually, but it's a lot harder to convince my heart that not every man is going to leave me."

"Sounds familiar." My eyes snap up to meet hers.

"Mama, are you...?"

"Yes, I met someone a few months ago, but I, uh, may have pushed him away when things got too serious."

"Mama! Why didn't you tell me?"

"I'm embarrassed for one that, at my age, I still haven't figured this all out. But now, talking to you about it, I realize I need to reach back out to Charles, see if there's still a chance we could work things out. Clearly, I need to set a better example of keeping my heart open and not letting fear win." She raises her eyebrows in a challenge, and I sink into my chair. "What do you say, Annie Lou? Maybe it's time for the Martin women to put a little faith in the happily ever after."

Chapter Sixteen

Eric

I SENSE ANNIE HOLDING back, but I'm so goddamn happy to be with her I haven't brought it up. It's not all the time that I feel her hesitating. Most of the time when we're together, she's in the moment, but every so often a cloud seems to pass over her eyes, and I can see her spiraling.

I don't blame her. It makes sense that she still doesn't quite trust me after everything we've been through. We spent so many years as enemies, treating each other so badly that sometimes I'm still shocked at how far we've come. If the last month and a half has taught me anything, it's that I'll do whatever it takes to keep Annie in my life.

Every day, I fall a little more in love with her, and I want the future I can clearly see: us together for the long haul. She may not trust me, trust us, yet, but I have enough blind faith for the both of us. I even started researching what it would take to get my PT license switched over to Illinois, in case she goes back to working in Chicago.

I'm all in.

But she's not quite ready to hear that, so I do my best to show her. Leena and Jessie have been lifesavers in giving me all the insider information. I order her favorite lunches regularly and I have plans to surprise her with a bouquet of her favorite flowers on the month anniversary of us becoming an official couple next week. Leena and I even cooked up a surprise for tonight's open mic night.

I walk into the Songbird to find Annie sitting at the bar, chatting with Fred. Her head is thrown back, laughing at something the older man says, and my heart flips in my chest. She's so beautiful, with her hair down and curled around her shoulders. She's wearing a soft-looking sweater dress and those fucking knee-high boots she knows drive me crazy.

I pop over to them and put my hand on her back. She turns in her seat and gives me a blinding smile.

"Speak of the devil, we were just talking about you," she says with a look of pure mischief on her face. Fred chuckles under his breath.

"Oh really? Telling Fred what an amazing boss I am?"

"Of course. We wouldn't possibly be talking about how much of a disaster your bookkeeping was."

Fred lets out a laugh. "It was pretty bad, son. I'm glad Annie Lou here could get you all straightened out." He claps me on the back and smiles. "Plus, it looks like the two of you were able to figure out that chemistry of yours. Nothing wrong with a little office romance to help pass the dreary January days."

He shoots us a wink as Annie chokes on her drink. I pat her gently on the back as she recovers.

"How did you know? I didn't say anything about us being together," she finally coughs out.

"I could tell by the way you talked about him. Plus, you both lit up like the Fourth of July when you saw each other just now. A blind man could see what's happening between you." Fred smirks and takes a drink of his water. "Are you still planning to go back to Chicago?"

The question makes me hold my breath. We haven't discussed Chicago in a couple of weeks. Last time we talked, she didn't know what she wanted to do. I haven't wanted to bring it up again, despite how curious I am to know where her head is at.

"Umm, I haven't fully decided yet. I hate the idea of going back, but I also hate to give up on the career I've built." She shrugs, peeling the label off her beer and avoiding eye contact with both of us.

"Hmm. I can see that being a tough decision," Fred says carefully, glancing back and forth between us. "I may have another career option for you to consider, Annie Lou."

"I'm open to suggestions," she murmurs, with a wave of her hand, urging him to continue.

"Many of my clients haven't been happy with the other accounting options here in Fort Starling. Mostly those big chain places that crank out as many tax returns as they can without getting to know their clients. Closing my practice left a bit of a void. If that was something you were interested in, I could help you get your own practice going and help you make connections."

Annie is quiet for a long moment as she thinks through everything Fred laid out. "I'll definitely consider it, Fred. Thank you." She stands up to hug the old man and looks up at me.

"If you go that route, you already have your first client," I say, smiling down at her.

"Well, yeah, you can't be trusted with your own bookkeeping," she scoffs.

Fred chuckles and pats me on the back. "She's not wrong, son. Now, if you'll excuse me, kids, it looks like Leena is ready for me on the stage."

We watch as Fred marches his way up to the stage. It's only then that I realize he's wearing a sparkly white western-style jumpsuit complete with bedazzling and fringe.

Fred takes the stage to thunderous applause and whistles. He launches into a rowdy version of "Friends in Low Places" that would either make Garth Brooks proud or embarrassed by the way this grandfather of seven is shaking his fringe-covered ass.

Annie and I freeze and lock eyes for a moment before bursting out laughing. Once we finally get ourselves under control, the chorus hits, and Fred dances, shaking his ass, and thrusting his hips. We lose our composure again, unable to watch the old man we both respect, hip thrusting.

Annie wipes tears from the corners of her eyes as she laughs up at me, and I'm so tempted to tell her I love her right then and there. Reaching out, I tuck her hair behind her ear as she smiles. I lean in and kiss her, reveling in the press of her body against mine in the busy bar. I want to tell her everything, but I'm struggling to get the words out.

In the end, I chicken out on actually saying the words and decide the song Leena and I have planned for later will have to be enough. For now.

TOWARD THE END OF the night, Leena nods me over. It's my turn for open mic, and I have a surprise for Annie. I've been planning it for a while. Now that it's here, nerves take over my body. I let out a shuddery breath and Leena smiles up at me.

"You're gonna do great. Annie will love this. Trust me, that album was on repeat when we were in high school."

"I just need her to know how much I care about her, but I also don't want to spook her, you know?"

"I know." Leena pats me on the arm and hops up onto the stage to introduce me. She sits at the keyboard and waves me over. "Alright, everyone. Give a warm welcome to my friend Eric, who's gonna sing a little Saving Jane for you."

I take my place at the microphone and swallow hard, before finding Annie still in her seat at the bar. She's smirking up at me, knowing I chose Saving Jane for her. Leena plays the intro for "Come Down to Me" and I start singing the slow, emotional ballad.

I watch Annie's face change as the lyrics of the song sink in. She visibly flinches at the line with the "L" word in it, and I start to sweat.

Fuck. She's going to freak out. I can see it on her face as I finish singing the song. I knew there was a possibility the song would send her spiraling, but I hoped, since I wasn't outright saying the words directly to her, it would be a more subtle way to go about it.

We finish out the song, and the crowd generously claps and cheers, but I'm focused on Annie and the distant look she has in her eyes as I approach. She gives me a smile as I take the stool next to hers, but it doesn't reach her eyes.

"You guys were great!" she says. Her voice has a hollow ring to it.

"Thanks, sweetheart." Silence settles between us. I can see in her eyes that she's spiraling, but I don't want to talk about it here in public. "You ready to head out?"

She avoids meeting my eyes as she peels her beer label. "Um. I think I'm just gonna head upstairs and sleep here."

I'm not even a little bit surprised she's trying to retreat. The real mystery is what I should do about it. Do I confront her about it? Do I let her slink away tonight and try again tomorrow? She doesn't give me a chance to respond.

"I'll see you at work in the morning." She leans over and kisses my cheek before booking it behind the bar and into the back. I stare at the place she disappeared, like she's going to suddenly reappear.

"You're going after her, right?" Jessie has sidled up next to me at the bar and is studying my face.

"I don't know, Jess." I let out a big breath and tug my hands through my hair. "She obviously wants space. Shouldn't I give it to her?"

"Sure, if you want that space to be permanent." I raise my eyebrows and indicate for her to continue. "She's scared, so she's hiding from her feelings. The more space you give her now, the more she'll convince herself she's doing the smart thing by running, by pushing you away. There's a reason she usually goes for emotionally unavailable dickbags. That way, she never has to actually put her heart on the line."

I nod and take in what she's saying. "What if she doesn't feel the same way I do, and she's avoiding the conversation?"

Jessie rolls her eyes so hard, I'm borderline worried she's going to hurt herself. "Come on, man. Don't do that. Do you really think deep down that she doesn't feel the same?"

With another pull of my hands through my hair, I think about her question. I replay the last month we've had together. Yes, Annie's been holding back, but is that because she's not in love with me, or is it because she is?

"Alright, Jess. I'm going up."

"Thank God. I thought I was gonna have to kick your ass for a second!"

I laugh and shake my head before downing the rest of my drink. As I mount the steps to Annie's apartment, I take slow, deep breaths, as if I'm about to go to battle. I guess I kind of am. I give the door a few loud knocks and wait. She has to know I'm the only one who would have followed her up here. After a few seconds of silence, I knock again, harder this time.

Annie pulls the door open with a panicked look on her face. She blinks, and I can see her expression shut down as she attempts to hide her fear. "Oh, hey. What's up?" she asks, pretending to be casual.

"We're really not going to talk about it?" I say as I walk into her apartment. Not that long ago, we were in these exact positions. Her hiding and me trying to figure out what the fuck she's thinking. A lot has happened between us since then, and I'm not going anywhere until she hears me out.

"Talk about what?" she asks with a wobble in her voice. Her bravado is slipping.

"Why you're up here hiding instead of going home with me, for starters? Come on, Annie, you haven't slept here in almost a month. What's got you rattled?"

"I'm not rattled. I just wanted to sleep here."

"Bullshit. You're freaked out by the song I picked, and you're hiding."

She crosses her arms and glares at me, but doesn't say anything. I glare back, surprised to find myself pissed off. She's purposely trying to push me away, and I am not a fan. We continue our stare off, each waiting for the other to fold until finally she shrugs and huffs out a breath.

"So what? Is this where you get pissed at me for not instantly falling into your arms? For having doubts? Where you decide I'm not worth the trouble?"

I stare for a long moment. She actually thinks that's what's coming next, and she's trying to brace herself. It makes me want to punch every single asshole who ever made her feel like she wasn't enough.

"Well?" she asks, losing her patience with my silence.

"Annie. This isn't a romance novel where I storm out, only to realize I can't live without you a week later."

"I know it's—"

"I already know I don't want to live without you," I cut off whatever she was going to say. "From the moment we met, you changed me, changed what I was looking for. Even when I was trying to convince myself I hated you, every other woman I've tried to date has come up short. Because they weren't you. Annie, I love you. I think maybe I've always loved you."

She's frozen in place as she studies my eyes, tears streaming down her face.

I approach her slowly, carefully, like I don't want to startle her.

"What if you've just built it up to be more in your head?"

"Pretty sure the last month has only convinced me more that you're the one I want."

"What if the IRS comes back with bad news? What if I didn't fix it right? You could lose your practice, and it would be my fault. How could we stay together after that?"

"If I lose my practice, it will suck, but it will be my own damn fault for not paying better attention. It wouldn't be on you. You've done everything you could to help me fix it, but if it's too late, I can accept that. I can get a PT job somewhere else, either here or in Chicago."

Her eyes go wide at that. "You'd move to Chicago for me?" she says in a whisper.

I run my hands down the sides of her arms and duck my head to make sure she's looking me in the eye.

"Sweetheart, I'd walk to hell and back for you. I spent over twelve years trying to get you out of my head, out of my heart. It's clear to me now that you belong there. I'm not fighting it anymore." I reach up to cup her cheek, tucking her hair behind her ears. Her caramel eyes are a dark, stormy brown, glassy with tears. "If you don't feel the same, if you don't see yourself having a future with me, I'll let you go. But I'm not gonna stand by and watch you push me away because you're scared. You're not just 'worth the trouble', you're worth everything."

She searches my eyes, brow furrowed. Her hands travel up my chest and loop behind my neck, running her fingers through the hair at my nape, sending chills down my spine. She pulls me down and crashes her lips into mine.

That's gotta be a good sign, right?

Chapter Seventeen

Annie

THIS MAN. *THIS MAN.* The one who used to be the bane of my existence, my biggest enemy, is declaring his love for me. The terrified girl in me wants to doubt him, but I know deep in my soul he's being sincere. It's time to push away my doubts and fears, and childhood trauma. It's time to trust him, fully and completely. To give him my heart, because he's only going to take care of it.

I pull back away from devouring him to gaze into his eyes again. "Eric, I am scared. I have never felt for anyone else what I feel for you. I've been hiding from it for years, because if I didn't let it in, then I couldn't be devastated by you walking away."

"I'm not—"

"I know. I'm scared, but I'm also in love with you. If there was anyone trustworthy enough to give my heart to, it's you. It's always been you."

He lets out a huge breath, all the tension he was holding in his muscles easing. "Oh, thank God."

"I'm sorry I doubted you."

"It's alright, sweetheart. I get it. And for the record, I'm scared too," he says in a soft voice, stroking a thumb across my cheek, wiping away my tears.

"Yeah?"

"Yeah. I think that's part of loving someone so much, always being varying degrees of afraid to lose them. I think that's what makes it worth it."

I can't help myself. I launch myself into his arms, picking up where we left off moments before. He boosts me up, and I wrap my legs around his waist as he carries me over to the bed in the corner. He sets me on my feet for a moment to pull my dress over my head, leaving me in the new red lacy bra and panty set I put on with him in mind before coming to open mic.

His eyes darken as he takes in the lingerie and skin on display. I had already ditched my boots when I came upstairs, leaving my legs bare. His gaze travels up and down my body several times as my temperature rises. The hunger in his eyes has my core throbbing, the ache burning through my abdomen.

"You are stunning. I could stare at you forever, sweetheart." My face flushes at the compliment. He leans into my body, hands resting on my hips. He nibbles on my earlobe before adding, "I could stare forever, but your body is the least interesting thing about you. Your fiery spirit, your kind heart, your fucking impressive mind: those are the things that make me want to keep you forever."

"Well, I guess I'll just put that dress back on..." I trail off, teasing him.

"Don't you dare," he says with a growl.

"I love you."

"I'll never get tired of hearing you say that. I love you too, sweetheart."

He captures my lips again, and the time for words is done. I pull at his clothes, and we break apart long enough for him to pull his shirt over his head. I yank at his belt buckle, impatient to get rid of the layers of fabric between us. We frantically strip, and when he's gloriously naked, I push him back onto the bed. He sits on the edge, peppering kisses along my belly and the underside of my breasts.

I straddle his lap as he runs his tongue along the edge of the lace of the bra I still have on. He quickly unclasps it, tossing it on the pile of our discarded clothing. He pulls my already puckered nipple into his mouth, and I gasp as he bites down gently.

"Eric. I can't wait. I need you." Reaching between us, I line him up at my entrance, and lower myself onto his length. I'm so full this way, as he bottoms out and I'm fully seated in his lap.

"Jesus, Annie. I'm not gonna last long."

I rock my hips, riding him in earnest, and he lets out a long groan. He grips my hips, helping me to rise and fall, meeting me with thrusts of his hips that shoot sparks through my veins. My inner walls start to spasm around him. He grabs my face and kisses me deeply.

It sends me over the edge, and I come *hard*, unraveling completely in his arms. He quickly follows me with his own orgasm. We stay like that for several long moments, clutching each other, face to face.

"I love you so much," he rasps out, resting his forehead against mine.

It takes my breath away to hear the naked emotion in those words. There's no going back from here, no more guarding my heart or trying to protect myself. I'm all in.

"WHAT THE ACTUAL FUCK is this?" I mumble to myself as I check my email the next week.

"What?" Eric asks, on alert from my bewildered and pissed off tone.

"It's an email from the managing partner at my job in Chicago, who also happens to be Kevin's mom. It makes no sense."

He leans over my shoulder to read the email that I've already read three times, trying to understand what's happening.

"What does she mean she was sorry to hear about your mom's illness? Your mom's doing great post-surgery."

"I have no idea what she's talking about, and she wants me to come to the annual appreciation dinner the first weekend of February. Why would she 'hope to see me there' if they're trying to push me out? I don't get it."

"Did you talk to her about the longer leave? Or just Kevin?"

"Just Kevin, but he... Oh my fucking god! That asshole. The partners didn't want me to take an extended leave. *He did.* He's been lying to everyone, banking on us not speaking to each other."

"That's the only thing I can think of that makes sense."

I sit back in my chair, trying to get a handle on the rage filling my body. I'm so pissed that yet another man has manipulated me, I'm seeing red.

"Whatcha thinking, sweetheart?"

"I'm thinking I'm going to Chicago next week. You wanna go with me?"

"I'm there."

He shoots me a grin, and some of the tension in my body eases. No matter what happens while we're in Chicago, I know one thing for sure: I don't want to live there anymore. I want to live here in Fort Starling with my friends, my mom, and the love of my life.

"Good, I'll need help packing up my apartment."

Eric's eyebrows shoot into his hairline. He hasn't pressured me to give an answer on whether I want to stay in Fort Starling, but of course, that's what he's hoping for. "Does that mean—"

"Yes. I'm moving back to Fort Starling permanently. Everyone I love is here." I shrug. It should have been so obvious before. I'm proud of the career I built in Chicago, but it never made me as happy as I've been here at home with my favorite people.

"What are the chances I can convince you to just move in with me?"

"Hmm. It does seem silly to move all of my things from my Chicago apartment into the Songbird when I almost never stay there."

"It does."

"Well, that settles it. If you're sure; it seems kind of fast."

"Yeah, it's fast if you don't count twelve years of pining."

I let out a laugh at that. He's right, it's not like we just met a few months ago. We've known each other our entire adult lives, both of us watching the other grow up from a distance, pretending the attraction and connection we felt was hate.

"So what's this appreciation thing we're going to?"

"It's a catered dinner they do in the office in early February. They like to do it far enough after the holidays but before the craziness of later in tax season. It's always been a fun night. Everyone gets dressed up, and there's an open bar and a live band."

"Got it. Sounds like a good time. So what's the plan?"

"I've got some thoughts, and it's definitely going to be a good time."

I give him a devious smile. I've got some phone calls to make and emails to send before we go to this party. They say the best revenge is moving on and being happy, and we're totally going to do that. But I'm going to nail Kevin's ass to the wall first.

ERIC AND I WALK into my office building on the night of the party looking like a goddamn power couple. Eric's wearing a perfectly tailored suit that he wears when he occasionally travels with the Flash players to away games. He looks so good in it, I'm almost distracted from our mission here. Almost.

Leena and Jessie went shopping with me to find a dress that is office appropriate but still makes my ass and boobs look incredible. I want Kevin to see what he's missing right before he gets the ass kicking of a lifetime.

We walk into the main office area to find my co-workers milling around with drinks and small plates of food. Several of them nod at me and give me polite smiles as we make our way through the party.

Our office is set up with an open concept, so it's usually a large room full of desks, but now most of the desks have been rearranged to the sides to create a more open space. One of the glass-walled conference rooms has been set up with a buffet that smells amazing. A bar sits in one open corner while a band is playing softly in the opposite corner.

My friend Keri waves from the bar. We've never been especially close. I didn't do a very good job of making friends here, but she's been an enormous help in gathering evidence over the last week. I wander over to her and give her a quick hug. She's wearing a stunning black sheath dress that dips low in the back and has her brown hair twisted up in a fancy-looking knot.

"Hi Keri, you look gorgeous! This is my boyfriend Eric."

He shakes hands with Keri and her husband.

"Girl, you're a fucking bombshell. Kevin's gonna shit his pants. What an idiot."

I grin at her. I wish I had gotten to know her sooner, because she's amazing. "Promise me we'll stay in touch? Just because I'm leaving Chicago doesn't mean we can't be friends."

"Absolutely." She squeezes my hand and shoots me a wink. "Hey, if you want to meet with Catherine, she's in her office. Might be a good time before things get wild here."

"You're right. Seriously, thank you for all of your help."

"It was no problem. Most of us can't stand Kevin. We were always on your side. I'll never forget you screaming at him over there by the copier." She laughs as I feel my cheeks heat. Me and my fucking temper.

"Maybe not my finest moment," I mumble.

"It was awesome."

"I'll see you after." I give her arm a squeeze and smile at her as Eric and I make our way toward one of the corner offices. As we get close, I see Catherine standing at her desk, reading a memo.

She's older, probably in her early sixties, but you'd never know it thanks to expensive skin care and a talented plastic surgeon. Her long brown hair is perfectly coiffed into a smooth updo. She's dressed for the party, clearly taking a few minutes to check on work before she joins the festivities.

She has a certain grace to her movements, but she can also be a total shark when she's making deals. I've always looked up to her so much. I'm not sure how Kevin turned out the way he did. I take a deep breath before approaching, gathering my courage.

"You got this, sweetheart. I'll be right here with you." He squeezes my hand and smiles down at me. What would I do without this sweet, gorgeous man? I give him a nod and walk up to Catherine's door and give it a quick knock, despite the door being open.

"Annie! Oh, I'm so happy you could make it. We miss you around the office. How's your mom doing?" She looks genuinely happy to see me and concerned for my mom, confirming that she knows nothing about Kevin's plot to push me out.

"My mom's great, Catherine. In fact, it seems there was some kind of miscommunication, because my mom's been doing well ever since her second knee surgery in early December. She was down for a few weeks, but after that, the recovery's been awesome."

"I don't understand. I thought you took extra leave because her health was poor and she needed you to take care of her."

"It seems you've been misinformed. I only intended to take three weeks of leave. Kevin insisted I take a longer leave." I let that statement settle in the air for a beat. "In fact, he said it was your idea that I take more time to make sure I, and I quote, 'really had my heart in this business.' I didn't want to take extra leave, but he forced it."

Catherine stands still for a moment before sinking down into her chair, pinching the bridge of her nose. "Why would he do this?" she asks, sounding defeated.

I'm a little startled she's not defending him, but I continue with my explanations. "I'm not sure if you were aware, but Kevin and I had a very short... romance... last year. It didn't end well. He quickly started dating Serena.

"I won't deny I was completely unprofessional in confronting him here at the office about his dismissal. I believe I embarrassed him with my, um, comments, and after that, he slowly started moving my accounts to Serena."

I look back at Eric, and he nods. I reach into my bag and produce the file folder I spent the last week compiling.

"This file is as much evidence as I could gather. A large amount of our disagreements were verbal, so I don't have proof of them, but you'll see the records of my clients being moved to Serena, a signed affidavit of my experience, as well as several affidavits from other co-workers detailing instances they witnessed inappropriate behavior from Kevin. I've also filed a formal complaint of sexual harassment and retaliation with HR, along with my resignation."

Catherine lets out a huge breath as she flips through the file. She shakes her head as she closes it. With a pained look on her face, she grimaces and asks, "Why didn't you come to me? With any of this?"

I shrug. "With all due respect, you're his mother. I didn't have a lot of faith that nepotism wouldn't win out. He also made it appear that many of these decisions came from you. I was hoping to keep the career

I worked so hard to build, despite my poor choice of romantic partners. If I complained, I was afraid I'd be out for sure."

She sighs. "I'm so sorry. Both that you had to experience this kind of harassment and that you felt you couldn't trust me. I promise I won't take your accusations lightly."

"That's all I ask. Thank you."

I nod and exit the office with Eric on my heels. He grins down at me.

"You were awesome in there, Annie. I'm so fucking proud of you for standing up for yourself."

"Thank you for being here with me. I love you." I push up on my toes and give him a chaste kiss. I'll save my true shows of gratitude for when we're out of this building. "Now, let's get some food, and then, I want to dance with my super-hot boyfriend."

"You've got yourself a deal, sweetheart."

Chapter Eighteen

Eric

I spot Kevin the second he enters the party. He's hours late, like the true asshole he is, and I don't have to be introduced to him to know it's him.

He's tall, maybe about an inch shorter than my six-two, with dark brown hair. I'll admit to him being a good-looking guy, but I can tell he's an asshole from his smarmy expression. He walks in with a blonde woman who is showing off way more cleavage than is appropriate for an office party.

Annie is chatting with her friend Keri when he spots her and stiffens. He's clearly angry to see her here. He really thought she'd quit quietly and never come back. My body tenses for a fight as he approaches us. Annie tenses as she notices him, too, and I give her hand a quick squeeze. I'll follow her lead, but I swear to god, I'm not afraid to punch this guy if it comes down to it.

"Annie. I'm surprised to see you here," the dickbag says, before giving her a sleazy smile. "I thought you were resigning."

Annie straightens her spine and fixes him with a vicious glare. She adds a devious smirk, and a chill goes down my spine. In all the time we pretended to hate each other, she never looked at me like that. It's kind of frightening and borderline arousing.

"I did resign. Tonight, in fact. I actually had a long conversation with Catherine about my reasons." She smiles her evil grin again, and the smile drops off Kevin's face. "I'd say it was nice working with you, but we both know that's a lie. If I ever see your slimy, arrogant face again, it will be too soon."

She turns and gives Keri a hug and nods to a few other coworkers. She smiles up at me and grabs my hand.

"Let's get out of here."

I smile and squeeze her hand. "Anything you want, sweetheart."

She doesn't even spare a glance for Kevin as we walk toward the elevators. We stop when we hear Catherine's sharp voice ring out across the office.

"Kevin. My office. Now."

We both turn to watch a confused-looking Kevin walk into his mother's office. She makes eye contact with Annie, giving her a quick nod before following him into the office and closing the door.

Annie grins up at me and raises her eyebrows as the elevator arrives, and we enter. When the doors close behind us, Annie lets out a huge breath and sinks against the back wall of the elevator. I lean over her with my hands on either side of her head.

"That went better than I expected," she sighs, relieved of the tension she had been carrying since we entered the office.

"You were incredible."

"I couldn't have done this without you."

"Yes, you could have, but I'm glad I was here to witness it."

Her smile is blinding as she pushes up on her toes and kisses me. "How about we get some champagne and head back to my apartment?"

"That sounds perfect to me."

"Good. It'll be nice to have some orgasms in that apartment that weren't self-made before saying goodbye to it."

I huff out a big laugh at that, and we exit the elevator hand in hand.

"I will be happy to make that happen, and trust me, it'll be better than nice."

She shoots me a wink as we leave the office building and head out into the icy February wind. It's freezing, but I'm already burning up for the gorgeous, strong woman beside me.

WE'RE PACKING BOXES THE next day when there's a knock at Annie's apartment door. Through the peephole, I see Catherine standing on the other side. I call out for Annie to come to the door as I pull it open, and she gives me a small nod of recognition.

"We weren't introduced last night. I'm Catherine Taylor." She holds her hand out for me to shake.

"Eric Reynolds, Annie's boyfriend," I offer with a friendly handshake.

She smiles and turns toward Annie as she joins us.

"Hi, Catherine. This is a surprise." Annie smiles politely, but her eyebrows are raised in question.

"Yes, well, I was hoping we could talk. I don't like the way things were left last night."

Annie nods, gesturing to the couch. "Of course, excuse the mess. We're just getting things packed up for the movers that will be here tomorrow."

"Right. So, you're planning on moving?" Catherine asks in a disappointed voice.

"I am. Over my extended leave, I realized I am much happier back home in Fort Starling." Annie shoots a wink and a smile at me as I continue to quietly pack up the books she has in the living room. I want to give them privacy, but still be here if Annie needs me.

Catherine sighs. "That's disappointing, but I understand. I had hoped you would come back to work for me. The position of managing director has just become open, and I was hoping to extend it to you."

Annie studies the older woman for a moment. "Kevin's position?"

"Yes. Kevin is no longer employed by the firm."

"You fired your own son?" Annie exclaims, eyebrows shooting up in shock.

"I had my suspicions that he wasn't a good fit for the culture that I want to promote at the firm. He's had several chances to fix certain behaviors, although nothing as bad as what he put you through. He wouldn't have gotten so many chances if he weren't my son, but unfortunately, it took me too long to do the right thing. I want to apologize again for how you were treated."

"Thank you, Catherine. And I'm sorry, but I have to decline the job offer. My time in Chicago is done. I'm ready for a fresh start."

"Understood. I feared that might be the case, so I've drawn up a severance settlement for you. I refuse to let you leave empty-handed, and you are welcome to reach out if you ever need a recommendation."

Catherine hands Annie a file folder of documents. Her eyes go wide at whatever she reads inside.

"Catherine, this is..." She blows out a big breath before continuing. "This is too much. I'm happy to know Kevin has been held accountable. I don't need a settlement."

"Use it as a cushion until you find your next endeavor. I will have the funds wired into your direct deposit account, and I refuse to take it back." She smiles warmly at Annie.

Annie stares back at her, stunned and shaking her head. "Thank you, Catherine."

"You're welcome. You take care." She pats Annie on the knee and walks to the door. She gives me a smile and a nod before she leaves. Annie is still sitting on the couch, staring into space.

"You okay, Annie?" I ask after she doesn't move for a solid minute. I plop down onto the couch next to her.

"Yeah," she says breathily. "I...she...it's a big number." She swallows hard before handing me the folder. I flip through the document to find the settlement amount. I let out a low whistle.

"That's a lot of zeros, sweetheart." I smile down at her. "Looks like you have plenty of time to decide what you want to do for work. You can do anything you want."

The stunned expression on her face fades as the options start to fill in. "You're right. But right now, I just want to go home."

"Right now? We only have half of your stuff packed." I glance around at the chaos. She looks around for a moment and then looks up at me as a shy smile takes over her face.

"True, but now I have plenty of money to hire the movers to do the packing, too. Let's go home."

"Works for me."

We grab our overnight bags, and Annie packs up a small box of her most important possessions. She takes a long look around before we leave the apartment and get back into my car for the six-hour car ride home.

As we leave the city, I reach over and give her thigh a squeeze before I ask, "Will you miss living here?"

She thinks for a long moment, searching her feelings. "Yes and no. I became an actual adult here. I'm happy I could have that independence. But it was also lonely, and working as much as I did, it was so fucking hard to make friends. I'll miss the hustle of a bigger city, but I'm ready to be back in Fort Starling for good."

"I'm glad about that, but if you ever change your mind, I'll go wherever you want to. I'm happy as long as we're together." I rest my hand on her thigh as we drive.

"Me too, Boss Man, me too." She places her hand on top of mine on her leg, and we enjoy the ride that way all the way home.

"Eric!" Annie shouts from the back office a week later. The urgency in her voice has me jogging back to see what's going on.

"What's wrong?" I study her, making sure she's okay. She's smiling from ear to ear, holding an official-looking letter.

"We did it!" she yells as she jumps into my arms.

"What did we do?"

"Here, read this," she says as she shoves the letter at me.

I read it twice to make sure I'm understanding it.

"If I'm reading this correctly, they've decided we only owe five thousand dollars in back taxes?" I look at her for confirmation.

"Yes. We'll add this documentation when we file your taxes for next year in April. I'm sorry I couldn't get them to erase it all."

She looks nervous, like she didn't just single-handedly save my business.

"Annie. Five K is nothing compared to what they originally said. It's doable and probably less than what I actually owe. You're a fucking miracle worker."

She laughs and blushes at the compliment. She shakes her head at me.

"We did this together. I never would have been able to get all the documentation together without you."

"I guess we make a pretty good team." I grin at her as she gets a surprised look on her face. "What?"

"We do make a good team. But I don't want you to be my boss anymore."

My heart stops. Is she quitting? "What? You don't want to work here?"

"I don't want to stop working here. I just don't want you to be my boss. I want to be equal partners. Let me buy into the practice. I can run the business and financial side, and you can focus on the therapy side without having to worry about spreadsheets and accounting software."

I laugh and run my hands through my hair, feeling like I've won the lottery. I kiss her and wrap my arms around her.

"Yes. Absolutely yes. But you don't need to buy in. I can give you half."

"Not a chance. As your business manager, there's not a chance in hell I will let you do that. We'll get an official valuation done on the practice, and I'll pay for my half. I have the money for this, and we can use the funds to upgrade equipment and give the staff raises."

"I love you so much." I cup her cheek and gaze into her eyes. "You've literally made my dreams come true. You saved my business, and now you want to be my partner in every sense of the word. You're everything I ever wanted."

"I love you, too." A mischievous glint takes over her eyes. "If I'm not mistaken, we don't have any more patients today?"

"No, we're done."

"Good. Send Amber home. I want to celebrate our new partnership the right way."

"Oh yeah? What did you have in mind?"

"Go let everyone go home, and I'll show you."

And she does. We christen the office with a couple of orgasms each before going home, only to fall into our bed for round three.

A man could get used to this. At home, at the office, I plan on showing Annie how much I love her every day for the rest of my life, no matter where we are.

Epilogue

Annie

One Month Later

"Okay, Miss Martin, you sign here, here, and here. Then it'll be your turn, Dr. Reynolds." The notary smiles up at us from looking over our partnership paperwork. After these are filed, we'll be official business partners.

I sign my name in all the spots she indicates and glance up to hand the pen to Eric.

"Here you go, Dr. Reynolds." His eyes flare with heat at my teasing tone. "I guess I can't call you Boss Man anymore now that we're partners."

He stalks closer to me and whispers in my ear, low enough that the notary can't hear him. "I can still think of some places where I'm the boss."

A chill runs down my spine in anticipation. We are *so* celebrating our new partnership the right way when we get home.

"I could get on board with that," I murmur back.

The notary finishes up the paperwork and shakes both of our hands in congratulations.

"Have a lovely day, Dr. Reynolds, Miss Martin." She gives us a polite nod and leaves the office. Eric studies me with a strange expression on his face for a long moment after she disappears.

"What?"

He searches my gaze again and shakes his head. "It's nothing, just a thought."

"Would you like to share your 'thought'?" I tease.

"Just...she called you Miss Martin."

"That happens to be my name."

He rolls his eyes. "I was wondering how you would feel about changing your last name...at some point."

"Oh yeah, what would I change it to?" I bite the inside of my cheek to stop the grin that wants to take over. I know what he's getting at, but I'm going to make him say it.

"Um...maybe you'd want to change it to Reynolds?"

"Jeez, man, I just moved in with you, now you want to get married?"

"I..." He freezes, his eyes narrow at me, suddenly realizing that I'm teasing him. I laugh out loud at the half-concerned, half-angry expression on his face. He shoots me a pouty look. "I was being serious, Annie."

Threading my arms around his neck, I play with the hair at the nape while his hands settle on my hips. "I know. I couldn't resist messing with you. But to answer your question... yes. I would be interested, at some point, in changing my last name to Reynolds."

The tension fades from his shoulders as he leans down to kiss me. "I'll keep that in mind."

"But for the love of God, let's get Leena and Bailey married first. I think Jessie's head would explode if we were both wedding planning at the same time."

He laughs at that, both of us knowing how crazy Jessie will get once we're deep into Leena's wedding planning. They're aiming for a late fall wedding, once the baseball season's over, so that they can take a long honeymoon. I can wait that long for Eric to propose. Probably.

"You're right. I'm sure Jessie's already a little stressed with Dan deciding not to retire at the last minute there. How did Jessie react?"

"I expected her to be furious, but when I texted her, she was really weird about it. She's coming over to help Leena and me get some things packed up before open mic, so I'm sure we'll get the full scoop then."

"When are you heading over there?"

I glance at my watch. "Not for...uh... another three hours. Why?"

His eyes darken as he squeezes my hips. "Because I have some plans for you, Miss Martin." He leans down to capture my mouth in a searing kiss, his tongue sweeping between my lips. He pulls me against him so that I can feel how hard he already is.

"Well then, take me home, Boss Man."

"THANKS FOR HELPING ME pack things up, Leens," I say as I close up another box. We're finally getting all of my stuff moved out of the Songbird apartment and into Eric's house. Getting the partnership drawn up for the practice and establishing my own freelance accounting firm has filled the last month since our trip to Chicago.

"No problem. It's not like I have anything better to do with Bailey gone," she says in a whiny voice. Spring training started a couple of weeks ago, so Bailey, Dan, and the rest of the Flash players are in Arizona for the next couple of months.

"Don't be grumpy. You're going to visit in a few weeks, anyway."

Leena sighs, "I know. But I got used to him being here all the time. I don't know what I'm gonna do with myself."

I chuckle at my friend, who insisted for years that she never wanted to be in another relationship. Look how far we've come.

"I'll be there to commiserate with you for those couple of weeks that Eric's with the guys." Nudging her arm, she sticks her tongue out at me. I'm hit with a renewed wave of gratitude that we can have these conversations in person. "Is Jessie still coming over? Did you get any more out of her about the non-retirement situation? She was super cagey with me the other day."

"Yeah, she said she was gonna come by after she got off the phone with Dan. She seemed weird, though. Something's definitely going on with them and has been for a long time."

"Hard agree. She's been acting weird for months."

A knock at the door announces Jessie joining us, almost like we summoned her.

"Speak of the devil, we were just..." My voice trails off as I take in the sight of Jessie. Her face is swollen, and her eyes are red and bloodshot. It's clear she's been crying. "Shit. Jess, are you okay?"

Jessie lets out a sob and crumples in on herself.

"Fuck," Leena murmurs under her breath as we both converge on Jessie.

"Jessie, what's wrong? Is Dan alright?"

Jessie sniffles and takes a deep breath. "Dan's fine. But I'm leaving him."

The silence in the room is palpable as we let her words sink in. We knew there was trouble brewing between them, but I would never have expected this.

Leena reaches for Jessie and tucks her into a hug. "What do you mean, you're leaving him? Like a divorce?"

"Um, yeah, I think so? Separation at least. I haven't thought about getting a lawyer yet, but I'm moving out while he's at spring training. Leena, I was hoping I could stay here until I figure out my next move? I just... can't be in that house by myself anymore, and I don't want to be there when he comes back. I'm... so tired of fighting and him not hearing me, not taking my feelings into account. I'm done."

Leena and I make eye contact over Jessie's head, both of us shocked into temporary silence. "Of course, you can stay here as long as you need," Leena says, recovering first and squeezing Jessie's arm.

"What can we do, Jess? What do you need?" I ask gently.

"Right now, I need shots and to sing some Taylor Swift."

"I think we can make that happen. We'll finish packing this stuff up tomorrow so we can get you moved in," I murmur, still sharing worried glances with Leena whenever Jessie's not looking. "How about you go get settled downstairs, and we'll shut everything down up here?"

Jessie nods and trudges back out the door. As soon as she's out of earshot, I turn back to Leena, panicked. "What the fuck do we do? *Shit.* I'm kind of freaking out, Leens."

"Why? Because our stable, happy, so-in-love-with-her-husband-it's-sickening best friend is having a total breakdown? Is that why you're freaking the fuck out?"

It makes me feel a little bit better, a little calmer, to find that Leena is also freaking out about this fresh development in our friend group. Like she said, Jessie has been the steady one for our entire adult lives. I take a deep breath to chill myself out before we need to go downstairs.

"Okay. We'll go down and have a fun girls' night where we will hopefully get the entire story from Jessie. We can see where we land from there. Either way, we're here for Jessie."

"You're right. I have Bailey doing some recon with Dan, but I told him not to say anything yet, just in case," she says as she slides her phone back into her pocket.

"Good plan. Alright. Let's go deal with our best friend's marriage meltdown."

The End

Thank you for reading The Boss Boycott! Want more Eric &
Annie? Scan here for a free bonus epilogue!

Curious about any of the music found in The Boss Boycott?
Checkout this playlist to find all of the songs mentioned as
well as a few extras!

Next Up

Jessie and Dan's marriage-in-crisis, second chance story is next in
The Marriage Meltdown.

See Where it Started

Turn the page to go back to the beginning with Leena & Bailey's
story in The Songbird Setup.

The Songbird Setup

Chapter 1

Leena

"I LOVE TO SING sad songs. For anyone who doesn't know me: I'm Leena, the owner of the Songbird Cafe and Bar. For those who are already familiar, this is old news, but for anyone new to our open mic night, I like to kick things off with this disclaimer." I laugh softly into the microphone.

The crowd chuckles, and some shake their heads, but they humor me. They know that if I perform at my cafe's open mic night, nine times out of ten, I will choose a slow, sad ballad.

Some of the most interesting songs to sing happen to be slow, heart-wrenching melodies, and I've always gravitated towards them. This is why going to karaoke nights with friends causes problems for me. Karaoke has this fun, crazy vibe, and nothing can kill the vibe faster than belting about lost love or singing a mournful song about heartbreak.

"My love of sad songs is exactly why, when I opened Songbird, I started open mic nights. I was tired of feeling left out at karaoke and just wanted to sing what I wanted to sing." I go on to detail the rules of our open mic nights.

"Rule #1: We do not tolerate heckling or booing of any kind. This is a safe space for anyone to perform whatever they want. Art is subjective. If you don't like someone's performance, use that time to visit the bar or the bathroom. It's the in-person equivalent of 'just keep scrolling.' Leave the mean comments for your social media feeds." I give the crowd a quick, serious-faced stare to make certain they understand that even though I'm cracking jokes, I'm dead serious about the rules, and in case there is anyone who thinks I'm kidding, I go on.

"Rule #2: We reserve the right to boot your ass if you break rule #1." I raise my eyebrows and make eye contact with a table of twenty-something guys that I haven't seen before. They nod their understanding and a couple of them hold up their hands in an expression of innocence, letting me know that they'll behave.

"Finally, rule #3: Have fun. This isn't life or death. Everyone will move on with their lives, whether you give the performance of a lifetime or completely forget every line of your new slam poem." I smile and the crowd chuckles. I sit down at the keyboard and lower the mic with me. "My final warning is that we do a lot of Broadway numbers here, and while you're welcome to do whatever you like for your turn—I'll never turn down anyone who wants to cover some Taylor Swift classics—show tunes are my jam and I play what I want!" I shrug my shoulders as I play the intro for "Burn" from *Hamilton.* Someone near the back whoops and I laugh into the microphone.

"Sounds like we've got some Lin-Manuel Miranda fans in the back," I sweep my gaze around the room, "Or maybe this is just the 'I've been cheated on and it sucks' anthem."

The laughter of the crowd gives me the same rush it always does. Laughter and applause are the best medicine and performing always helps me to become lighter and less haunted. I give myself over to that emotion as I launch into the song, wishing I could feel this free all the time rather than my default settings of melancholy and sarcastic.

The lift performing gives me is one of the main reasons that I often open and close the open mic night lineup. I like to give my speech about the rules and what to expect. I also like to say goodnight to the loyal customers who drank with us all night. Plus, I have very little social life, so the twice-a-week open mic nights get me out of my small apartment above the cafe and out of my head for a little while.

The Songbird Cafe and Bar is a large open rectangular room. The bar runs along the right side of the room with open back barstools along the front. Seating is a mix of cozy chairs and couches, with high-top tables scattered throughout the room. I wanted to create a place for anyone to hang out, no matter the time of day. We even have a few racks of donated new and used books that operate like a little free library along the left side of the room, for anyone looking for something to read while they relax in our comfy vibe.

Towards the back of the bar, we have a barista station that handles all the morning cafe drinks with a pastry case that we fill from local bakeries. A mirrored wall displays an assortment of liquor and mixers, and we offer a selection of local beers on tap for our evening crowd. Most people will bring takeout since we don't have a full kitchen.

The stage, complete with microphone, electric keyboard, and speaker system, sits in the left corner for our open mic nights. I bought a gently used karaoke setup from a bar that was going out of business to add options for open mic nights.

I started open mic nights about two months after opening Songbird. Morning coffee and pastry sales were good, but I wanted a reason for people to come out in the evening. I had the idea one weekend after some friends dragged me out for karaoke and I couldn't sing what I wanted without bringing down the entire room. In the year since, they've become increasingly popular and we always have a full crowd.

As I come to the end of "Burn," I let myself get a little lost in the lyrics and the thoughts of the past bubble up. It's been two years since my life blew up, but somehow the wounds are still fresh when I'm performing like this. However, there is something cathartic—like I'm working through some of the damage—when I get lost in the song lyrics.

After playing the final notes, the crowd applauds, and whoops and my spirit lifts. I take just a second to enjoy the moment and then I put the past back in the box in the back of my mind where it belongs.

"Thank you, everyone!" I say, hoping the sincerity in my voice is perceived by the crowd. "Next up we've got Stella and Ian to entertain us with their acoustic stylings." The singer-songwriter duo that's always popular with the crowd takes the stage and gets set up with their acoustic guitars. They start with a really cool cover of *NSYNC's "Bye Bye Bye" before launching into some of their original pieces. I hang out at the bar to listen for a little while and then continue on with my Tuesday night.

Later that week, I'm helping Cass tend the bar before the start of open mic. For a Friday night in early January, we're super busy. We've had an unseasonably warm week and more people are here without the snow and ice encouraging them to stay home. On top of that, we're short-handed tonight since our weekend bartender, Alaina, is out with the flu.

Cass is Songbird's full-time general manager and has been with me from the start. She is a total rock star when it comes to running the business side. We met in my junior year of college when she was a freshman. Cass and I hit it off right away back then, and she's become one of my best friends now that we're running Songbird together.

We reconnected after Cass finished her MBA from Ohio State. After she graduated, I asked if she wanted to help me open my own place. She grew up working in her family's restaurant in West Virginia and it gave her the perfect experience for running a cafe and bar. I prefer to focus more on the creative side of the business like fun events and the ambiance of the space.

Cass and I have only gotten closer during the year she's worked for me. Our personalities mesh perfectly and there's no one else I would want running my business. We're both snarky and fluent in sarcasm and inappropriate jokes. We like to joke that we are twins separated at birth, although we look nothing alike.

In appearance, we're total opposites, with her tall willowy frame and dark straight hair that is cut into a short, smooth bob framing her face perfectly. I'm several inches shorter with curves for days. I usually pull my unruly auburn curls up into a bun or Dutch braid to keep them out of my way.

"What depressing ballad are you kicking off open mic with tonight?" Cass murmurs with a smirk. She is not a fan of my penchant for sad songs and likes to remind me of that fact often. If Cass gets up to sing, she usually goes with something fun and upbeat—she has no problems fitting in at karaoke—although she loves show tunes as much as I do.

"I'm thinking it's a Sara Bareilles sort of night," I smirk as she rolls her eyes and sighs.

"Whatever floats your boat, boss-lady!"

"Thank you so much for your support." I snark back at her and laugh as I stroll up to the piano. I sit down and sigh, with tiredness weighing on my body.

A recurring nightmare featuring my asshole of an ex made for a night of shitty sleep. I woke up in a pool of sweat with my heart pounding. It took me a while to shake off the panic and rush of adrenaline. I had a hard time sleeping after that so I'm exhausted, emotionally drained, and downcast today. Sara Bareilles's songs are like my performance security blanket, always there when I need to let the emotions flow.

I run through my usual welcome speech with the rules of open mic night and start playing "Gravity" which is one of my absolute favorites.

This song has carried me through several heartbreaks and always feels relevant. I hear the door open as I start the second verse, but I don't bother looking up. People come and go a lot through open mic night and I prefer to let myself get lost in the lyrics.

As I come to the bridge, a chill runs up my spine, and I can sense someone watching from near the door. We dim the lights in the bar so I can't see him very well, only his very tall frame standing watching me sing. The hairs on my arm stand on end and my heart rate picks up. It reminds me a little of the adrenaline I experienced after my nightmare, but this time I'm not scared. I'm intrigued. I have never in my life been so aware of someone's physical presence in my life and I silently hope the tall stranger will stick around so I can figure out why. Maybe I know him?

After I finish my number and hand off the mic to the next act, I pop behind the bar to help Cass manage the crowd that has built up. I'm so focused on running drinks that when I look up and find the mystery man sitting at the bar in front of me, I'm almost startled. Not just because of the reaction my body seems to have to his presence, but also because he is stunning.

His dark wavy hair is close-cropped on the sides and worn a little longer on top. He has the perfect amount of scruff covering his chiseled jaw, somewhere between a five o'clock shadow and a full beard. His dark brown eyes have a spark of humor in them and follow me as I approach. Even sitting on the bar stool, I have to look up at him to get his order.

"Hi there! What can I get you?" I chirp, trying not to let on how his presence is affecting me. If he knew me at all, he'd see right through me. Most of my regulars are used to me being grumpy or snarky with them.

I rarely do the upbeat customer service voice but something about him makes me nervous.

He takes a glance at our beer list. "I'll take the Wolf's Ridge lager on tap, thanks," he answers with a smooth, deep voice and a smile.

"Be right back with that!" I take off to pour his drink at the other end of the bar with my hands shaking.

What the hell is wrong with me? He hasn't even said anything real, just ordered a beer, but my heart is beating like he asked me to marry him.

Whoa.. marry him? Where the actual fuck did that thought come from? I berate myself as I pour his beer. I'm not sure I believe in marriage anymore. I'm certainly not in the habit of imagining strangers proposing to me.

As soon as the thought crosses my mind, I picture it. This beautiful man, down on one knee, holding my hand and looking up at me in adoration. It's enough to make my stomach churn and I'm even more nervous as I head back towards him. I set the glass on a coaster in front of him as he slides a twenty across the bar.

"I'll just be right back with your change!" I slowly slide away as I'm talking. I want to both be near him and get as far away as possible at the same time, and it's scrambling my brain a bit.

"Nah, keep the change. " He gives me a small smile and my stomach bottoms out while my heart rate climbs.

"Oh! Thank you!" I give him a genuine smile despite my unease. Cass is saving up for a down payment on a new car and generous tippers are always welcome at my bar. I glance around for the next customer when I realize the line is slowing down and everyone has been helped. I start to walk away when the handsome stranger stops me.

"Wait! I ... uh ... I actually came over here to talk to you," he says in a rush. I raise my eyebrows at that and wait for him to elaborate. "I was walking past and heard you singing and I just had to find out where that voice was coming from." He finishes quickly, seeming mildly embarrassed by the confession.

"Well, I'll be damned," I quip. "I guess I owe some cartoon fairytale writers an apology!" The snarky comment makes me feel a little more like myself. My cheeks are blushing from his compliment, but I can't keep the sarcasm from flying out of my mouth.

"What do you mean?" He asks and I laugh while rolling my eyes before launching into one of my favorite tirades.

"Fairy tales completely set me up for disappointment when all the boys growing up didn't give two shits about my singing voice." I realize I'm about to confess an old insecurity, but I'm not able to stop myself. "For a chubby, awkward teenager who was way too into musical theater, the promise that my prince charming just needed to hear me sing to be interested definitely did not pan out the way I hoped." I laugh and only just barely keep the bitterness out of my voice.

The gorgeous stranger chuckles kindly and takes a slow up-and-down glance at my body that sets my skin tingling. After years of work on my self-esteem, I love—or at least feel some neutrality about—my mid-size curvy body. I no longer beat myself up about my pant size having double digits and I refuse to even own a scale.

But in the gaze of this stunning man, I'm feeling self-conscious. What is he seeing when he looks at me? I think I'm detecting a hint of heat in his eyes, and that makes me blush all over again. I'm sure he notices my cheeks burning but is nice enough not to mention it.

"Do you think your manager would mind if I bought you a drink?" He asks with a smile. He clearly missed the part of my welcome speech where I mentioned that I'm the owner of the bar. So I play along and pour myself a gin and Sprite.

"I don't think she would mind at all," I smirk as I sip the drink. He's just about to say something when the alarm on my phone goes off, making me jump. I look down at my watch to see that it's almost nine and time for my weekly FaceTime with Annie.

My two best friends and I have been a tight-knit trio since we met in the seventh grade. For years, it was Annie, Jessie, and me. We did everything together, all the way through college at Ohio State, before going our separate ways.

Jessie and I have found our way back to Fort Starling, but Annie moved to Chicago a few years ago and her job keeps her crazy busy. We've taken to scheduling our FaceTimes to make sure we stay in touch. I miss her big time, so I am not in the habit of bailing on our calls, but the handsome guy in front of me makes it tempting.

"Oh shit, I have a phone call I have to take!" I say apologetically.

That I even for a second considered blowing off Annie for this guy makes my stomach drop. What am I even doing? I'm not interested in dating anyone. I don't want a relationship. What is even the point of staying here chatting with him when I'm not interested in it going any further than a drink in my bar? He nods like he isn't sure whether I'm telling the truth or blowing him off, and for some reason, I can't stop myself from continuing our exchange.

"Will you be around for a while? I'll be back down to close out open mic at midnight." I hear the pleading tone in my voice that low-key embarrasses me, but can't quite make it stop. He checks his phone and shrugs a bit.

"I've got kind of an early morning, so I'm not sure if I can stick around," he says regretfully.

"Oh okay. Well... it was really nice to meet you!" I say too loudly and spin around. I take off through the door to the kitchen so he doesn't see the disappointment and confusion blazing across my face.

It's only as I'm climbing the stairs to my apartment over the bar that I realize we didn't even exchange names. He's still a mystery and that's probably for the best. I actually hope he's not there when I go back down to the bar. For the most part, I believe my own lies.

Scan here to continue reading!

Acknowledgements

Writing one book feels like a bucket list item that was super cool to cross off, writing two feels like the start of a new career. I couldn't have done any of it without a whole host of people who support me everyday.

Thank you to my husband, Blair, for your endless support, even if you still haven't read my books. I'm sure you totally will at some point...

To my boys for not complaining (much) when I have to focus and write instead of playing outside. Also, for inspiring Eric's childhood nickname.

Huge thank you to my editor, Lily Luchesi at Partners In Crime Book Services. You were awesome to work with and I can't wait for us to dive in on book three together!

My beta readers: Katie, Kaitlin, Jami, and Abby. Thank you so much for spending time reading my books and giving me your feedback. You guys give me the confidence to let other people read my work.

Forever thankful for my Fit4Mom Columbus North village, especially the Book Club mamas. Your support is priceless and necessary to my life.

Dill Pickle and Ranch Pringle Mingles for being salty snack perfection. Chocolate covered marshmallow eggs for being the sweet.

BIGGBY Coffee for regular caffeine and inspiring Annie's favorite drinks.

Last but certainly not least, the readers. Thank you, thank you, thank you for spending your reading time with me. It means the world to me that you chose my book!

Also by Maggie

The Songbird Cafe Series

The Songbird Setup (Leena & Bailey)

The Boss Boycott (Annie & Eric)

The Marriage Meltdown (Jessie & Dan)

About the Author

MAGGIE LINN SHARPE HAS been creating worlds and characters in her mind for as long as she can remember. Because no career path felt quite right, despite her efforts, and motherhood limited her social time, she decided to try writing a romance novel. Now she's pretty sure she won't be able to stop.

Maggie lives outside of Columbus, Ohio with her husband, her two boys, and her mother. When she's not writing, she's usually reading romance, obsessing about musicals, or spending time with her kiddos, which usually involves learning more than she wanted to know about Minecraft and watching Bluey on repeat.

Connect with Maggie

www.ingramcontent.com/pod-product-compliance
Lightning Source LLC
Chambersburg PA
CBHW020144120726
47903CB00007B/2407